"I'm a bawd," she said.

"A loose wench. I need you and I want you, so please don't say no. I'm terribly out of practice and my underwear isn't lacy. It's just cotton and mended, but I want you."

He put a firm and gentle hand on her mouth to keep her from talking. Then he kissed her and helped her off with her sandy dungarees and yellow T-shirt. Somehow, during all of this, he managed to steer her to the bunk and turn off the cabin light.

She remembered nothing about her past, she forgot about the terrible explanations tomorrow would bring, she only knew and understood what was happening to her with this stranger called Leo Rice. . . .

Fawcett Books
by John D. MacDonald:

- [ ] ALL THESE CONDEMNED   14239 $1.95
- [ ] APRIL EVIL   14128 $1.95
- [ ] THE BEACH GIRLS   14081 $2.25
- [ ] CANCEL ALL OUR VOWS   13764 $1.95
- [ ] CLEMMIE   14015 $1.95
- [ ] CONDOMINIUM   23525 $2.75
- [ ] THE CROSSROADS   14033· $1.95
- [ ] CRY HARD, CRY FAST   13969 $1.95
- [ ] THE DAMNED   13997 $2.25
- [ ] DEAD LOW TIDE   14166 $1.95
- [ ] DEADLY WELCOME   13682 $2.25
- [ ] DEATH TRAP   14323 $1.95
- [ ] THE DECEIVERS   14016 $1.95
- [ ] THE END OF THE NIGHT   14192 $2.25
- [ ] THE EXECUTIONERS   14059 $1.75
- [ ] A FLASH OF GREEN   14186 $2.50
- [ ] JUDGE ME NOT   14057 $2.25

Buy them at your local bookstore or use this handy coupon for ordering.

COLUMBIA BOOK SERVICE, CBS Inc.
32275 Mally Road, P.O. Box FB, Madison Heights, MI 48071

Please send me the books I have checked above. Orders for less than 5 books must include 75¢ for the first book and 25¢ for each additional book to cover postage and handling. Orders for 5 books or more postage is FREE. Send check or money order only. Allow 3-4 weeks for delivery.

Cost $_____   Name _____

Sales tax*_____   Address _____

Postage_____   City _____

Total $_____   State _____ Zip _____

The government requires us to collect sales tax in all states except AK, DE, MT, NH and OR.

Prices and availability subject to change without notice.   **8999**

the beach girls

by John d. MacDonald

FAWCETT GOLD MEDAL • NEW YORK

THE BEACH GIRLS

Published by Fawcett Gold Medal Books, CBS Educational and Professional Publishing, a division of CBS Inc.

ISBN: 0-449-14081-4

Printed in the United States of America

First Fawcett Gold Medal printing: September 1959

25 24 23 22 21 20 19 18 17 16 15 14 13 12

Contents

ONE

Captain Orbie Derr

IT WAS A RIGHT PRETTY EVENING when Leo Rice arrived at the Stebbins' Marina. Friday, it was. The first day of August. It was later on the same month that everything went to hell for just about everybody. Maybe he was, like Joe Rykler explained to me, a catalyst. But I've got the general opinion everything was due to go to hell anyway. Things had been working up to it. I won't deny he didn't have something to do with it. But it took more than just one man to ruin what Joe Rykler calls a way of life.

It was a fine evening. Breeze out of the east off the Atlantic, moving about four knots. A pink glow of sunset reflected on the quiet thunderheads out over the Atlantic.

A bunch of us were on D Dock, as usual, lounging around on cushions and chairs taken off the boats. Tin washtub full of ice and beer. I'd set my charcoal grill up on the dock and loaded it. Later on we'd light it and cook the 'burgs.

Me and Joe Rykler and Anne Browder and Christy Yale and Gus Andorian. Bud and Ginny Linder. Alice Stebbins, who owns the marina. Charterboat row is opposite D Dock, and on that evening Lew Burgoyne had come over from there and joined us. He captains the *Amberjack III*.

It was nice there, opening a beer once in a while, having a lazy argument about nothing at all, watching the night come on. The car lights were on over the other side of the Inland Waterway, going north and south on A-1-A, going back and forth across the hump-back bridge over Elihu Inlet. There wasn't much boat traffic up and down

7

the Waterway, and not much in the big Stebbins' Marina basin, just kids and old fellas running in to tie up their outboards over at A Dock where they keep the small stuff. On the other side of us, beyond the rickety old marina buildings, traffic moved slick and fast, whispering by north and south on Broward Boulevard. It made D Dock like an island, a special quiet place, water licking gently at the hulls of the tied-up boats.

I was looking out toward the Waterway when I saw the old Higgins Sedan, coming down slow from the north, make the turn in between the rickety markers on either side of the entrance to the basin. I saw right away that he was cutting the north marker too tight. It's silted-up there. You have to give it a lot of room, just like you do the black nun-buoys on your way out Elihu Inlet on anything less than half tide. I sucked in my breath and held it the way you do watching anybody about to go aground, but somehow he eased over and came on into the basin dead slow, heading for the T at the end of C Dock where the gas pumps are.

Everybody had stopped talking. We were all watching him. Old Billy Looby, who's been dockboy ever since 1919 when Jess Stebbins had bought the land and started out renting boats and selling bait, went trotting on out the length of C Dock past the cruisers of the winter residents who store them at the marina over the hot months.

The fella at the wheel of the Higgins give it a little reverse power on both engines to stop himself, then cut both engines. Sound carried good. We heard Billy yell, "You want gas?"

"No thanks. I'd like to tie up."

"For how long? Overnight?"

"Longer than that. Maybe a month."

Billy turned and stared over toward us and then yelled in his shrill old-man's voice, "Alice, this here fella—"

"I heard him," Alice bellowed. When she wants to let go you can hear her over on the public beach. "Put him in D-13."

"D-13?" Billy repeated blankly. He was as surprised as we were.

"Show him where it is and tell him to back it in."

As Billy was pointing and explaining, Joe Rykler said,

"Alice, you are dumping an inept stranger into our little community. What's wrong with B Dock where he can be happy with the rest of the tourists?"

"Rotten pilings which got to be replaced, busted dock boards which got to be replaced, and a creosote and cuprinol job. I got to have Billy and Bunny Beeman move what's already there. And who is running this god-damn marina anyhow?"

"You are, Alice. You are," Joe said.

There are fifteen slips along D Dock. Ten boats moored there. The permanent residents. Even though D-13 was the last one out toward the end—right next to Rex Rigsby's Bahamian ketch, *The Angel*—we all felt a sort of resentment that Alice was moving somebody in with us.

Billy had trotted back to shore and he went loping out D Dock to help the stranger with the lines. We get hardly any tide movement inside the basin, but I had a hunch the wind was going to bother the guy when he backed into the narrow slip between the pilings. Maybe there was somebody below to help him with the bow lines and fend the Higgins off the pilings, but I had another hunch he was alone.

I saw him ease around and make his swing. He made it too late. Just before he banged his transom into a piling, he went out again and started from further upwind. But he didn't have the smallest idea of how to use his props and rudders to swing the rear end of that boat. Billy was yelling instructions the guy couldn't hear over the sound of his engines. Billy is a mean little old son of a bitch, and I knew Billy would enjoy to see him foul up good. Give him something to feel superior about. So I got up and went on out to see if I could give him a hand.

He came in too fast, staring back over his shoulder. He gave the starboard piling a hell of a thump. I ran out the narrow walkway between the slips, made a flying leap and landed sprawling in the cockpit just as the man, unnerved by the thump, shoved the shift levers forward and moved back out again.

"Let me have it," I said. "Get the bow lines."

He gave up the controls willingly and went forward. The port engine was running ragged, and I could tell by the feel of the wheel the steering cable was frayed. I eased it back in, swung the bow left and right so he could slip a loop over both pilings, moved it back to the dock, yelled to him when to make the bow lines fast. I cut the engines. Billy and I rigged the two stern lines.

The man came back to the cockpit and, in what was left of daylight, I got my first good look at him. He was about forty, a big lean guy, deeply tanned, with one of those pleasant ugly faces. He wore khaki shorts and he looked as if he was in fine shape. But he didn't look sure of himself—I mean in more ways than not being able to handle thirty-four feet of boat. Like he'd been gutted. Like some of the running parts had been taken out of him and put back in with string.

He stuck his hand out. The palm was calloused. "I'm Leo Rice," he said. "I'm grateful to you. I had the feeling I was going to knock the dock over."

He spoke in a careful, educated way that didn't go with the calloused hand or the ropy brown muscles in his shoulders.

"Orbie Derr," I said. "Guess you're not used to boats."

"I bought this up in Jacksonville two weeks ago. They gave me a short course in navigation and boat handling. If there's anything I haven't done wrong yet, I can't think of it."

I didn't want to tell him that the first thing he did wrong was to buy the boat. I could tell it had had hard use and not much care. Somebody had fixed it up cheap and flashy for a quick sale. Slapped paint over the corrosion.

"Who do I see about arrangements to stay here?" he asked.

Billy spat into the dark water. "You plug in right here for electric. This is your meter. Better wrap your lines or you'll chafe 'em. Connect your hose here. Garbage can in the dock box there. You want supplies or laundry or ice or anything, you see me and I'll fix you up. The office is closed. You can check in in the morning. Dollar a day dockage, mister. Pay your own electric. No charge for water."

Billy and I left him there and walked back along the dock to the group. Billy snagged a beer, uninvited, opened it and took it along with him back to his little room in the end of the storage shed.

"What've we got, Orbie?" Christy Yale asked in her funny, husky voice.

"A waterborn damn fool name of Leo Rice in an old crock of a Higgins he got stuck for in Jax. Didn't change the name. It's called *Ruthless*. Nice-spoken fella about forty, traveling alone. But he don't know a winch from a wench."

"Now that's one thing I got a strong feeling about," Lew Burgoyne said.

"You got strong feelings about everything," Alice Stebbins said.

Lew ignored her. "Man has to have a license to drive a hundred-dollar car, but if he's got enough money to buy thirty feet of boat, he can go right on out and drown himself free of charge. Like the time that big Chris ran the hell right into me and I find out the guy owned it three days. Came from Kansas. Never saw water before."

We argued that back and forth. I started the charcoal going. We opened some more beers. It was full night. You could see the neon of the hotels over on the beach.

After a while they started kidding me, giving me a real ride about the next bunch of girls due in on Monday. It's the one part of the job like to drive me out of my mind. I got to live around boats. I was born down in the Keys. I'm thirty-five. I pretty much go my own way. Spent my life on the water, with a stretch in the Navy. Tried marriage once and didn't like it, and pulled out soon as I could. She remarried. Caught a rich tourist. Fine-looking woman.

Anyhow, I got this job five years ago, hired captain of the *Lullaby*, forty foot diesel Matthews, about all the boat one man wants to handle. I live in the next-door slip to the *Lullaby*, aboard my own houseboat named *Mine*. Bought her run down and fixed her up neat and pretty. The *Lullaby* is a corporation boat. Owned by the Bitty-Beddy Corporation up in Pennsylvania, biggest maker of cribs, highchairs and toidy seats in the world. It's a handy place to keep the boat, right here at Stebbins' Marina at Elihu Beach, Florida. You can run out the pass into the Atlantic in minutes. And the company also owns the Linda Lomas Motel, just four blocks from here, a block off Broward to the west.

11

It used to be the perfect job. I'd get a letter or a phone call or a wire, and some of the corporation boys and their guests would come down and we'd either use this as a base for fishing, or take a run down to the Keys or to Havana or over to Nassau. About a hundred days of work a year, not counting everyday maintenance.

Then last summer some smart guy up there in Pennsylvania decided that in the summer months they could run batches of women from the offices down here to stay two weeks in the motel and have the use of the boat. Real generous. It's a mess. I got four batches last summer, and this summer it will be five. Six to eight females in each batch. Maybe they're just fine up there, but they go crazy down here in the summer. They get drunk and they get seasick and they get sunburned so bad they get chills and fever. They run from twenty-five to fifty-five, and they aren't hired for looks. You should hear them all squeal at once when somebody hooks a fish. The better-looking ones sometimes seem willing enough, but I know damn well that if word ever got back to Pennsylvania that Captain Derr messed around with one of them, good-by job. I did take a chance one time last summer, on a little gal in the last batch, when I was wore down by it all. Red-headed, with hair the exact same shade as mine. She was so scared about me ever saying a word about it, I figured it was safe enough. She snuck aboard *Mine* three times and it was fine. She wrote one long sloppy letter about how she was going to be married three days after the day I got the letter, but I didn't answer it.

On Monday, the fourth, I was due for a new batch, the third of this season. The boys over in charterboat row think it's funny as hell telling me how good I have it, and will I change jobs and all that. The hell of it is, I like things neat. And it would make you cry to see what one batch of them can do to the *Lullaby* in just one day of cruising. Women are mostly so damn untidy.

It had been Christy's turn to buy the groceries, so when it was time she walked up to girl's town—Joe Rykler had named it that. It's just two houseboats moored side by side on the shore side of Rex Rigsby's ketch. Christy lives aboard the *Shifless* with Helen Hass, the sour little brunette job who runs the office and books for Alice Stebbins, and goes out to classes every night improving herself. Just beyond the *Shifless* is the twin houseboat, the *Alrightee,* where Anne Browder lives with Amy Penworthy.

Christy brought the food back and she and I unwrapped it under one of the feeble dock lights and then started the hamburgers cooking. Meat spitting over the fire, and that *pfisst* sound when a beer can is opened, and quiet talk there in the night.

Old Gus Andorian told us some funny steel mill stories we hadn't heard before. He's lived in an old motorless scow tied to D Dock for the past four years. He must be getting close to seventy, but he's big and thick and solid as a tree. He worked all his life in the mills. His wife died five years ago. From what he tells, she was a little bit of a thing, and she had strong ideas about drinking, swearing, spitting and gambling. She kept the lid on Gus. They raised six daughters, all married, and their first names all begin with A. Proper like their ma, I guess. Every one of them wants Gus to come live with them. And every once in a while one of them will make a trip down to talk him into living on shore. They don't have any idea how good a time Gus is having. He is making up for the sober years.

And there's one thing that every one of us regulars knows about, but never hints about. Gus and Alice. Alice Stebbins was Jess Stebbins' third wife. He buried the other two. He married Alice ten years ago, when she was about forty, I'd say. She'd come down on the insurance money from her husband, killed on a construction job in Ohio. And stayed, like so many do. Married Jess and buried him three years later. Was going to get the marina all fixed up but somehow never got around to it.

So she's fifty, and you never see her in anything but jeans and a man's shirt, and she's big without being soft. But the way she moves, soft and light like a lion, the way she can look at you, you know she's all woman, more woman than plenty of them half her age. She and Gus bad-mouth each other in public a lot, but there's a warmth under it. And everybody knows that every so often Gus will sneak up into that cramped old apartment over the marina office, clumsy and sneaky as a bear stealing a picnic, and climb into the big noisy old brass bed. It does no harm. When

13

she had the bad flu last year, Gus took care of her, gentle as a woman.

"Is coming down now that damned Annabelle," Gus rumbled. "Maybe next week. I got a card. Husband and kids too. 'Papa, please come live with us.' What they want—a baby sitter. Yah."

We polished off all the groceries and went back to the beer. The ice was all gone and you had to paw around in the ice water to find one of the few cans left. Bud and Ginny Linder were sitting close, as usual. They don't paw each other in public. But they sure sit close. They live aboard the *Free and Fancy,* a big custom schooner under maybe its fifth ownership. They started out from Maryland to sail her around the world, but about six miles off Elihu Beach, a year and a half ago, a little tornado on a clear day ripped the sticks out of her and smashed everything topside. Bud jury-rigged a spare jib and got her in. They're good kids. Bud now manages a gas station and Ginny works in an office-supply store. They've put every dime and every minute back into the *Free and Fancy.* But now Ginny is a little bit pregnant, so maybe they won't go around the world the way they still claim they will.

Along came one of those silences, and right in the middle of it, Judy Engly cut loose over across the way in charter-boat row. She's sort of a plump, sulky-looking little girl. Been married now to Jack Engly nearly three years. No kids. Jack skippers his own boat named *Judy's Luck.* They live aboard. When there's women in the charter party Judy crews for him. Otherwise he picks up one of the boys hanging around looking for a day of crewing.

Even when you know just what it is, it isn't so damn easy to take. I've seen tourists go right up in the air and land with their mouth open and their eyes bugged out. She starts low, like moaning, and goes on up until she's yelling at the top of her lungs. Then it goes up into a long screech like somebody's killing her and fades down like a siren into a sort of gurgle and some more moanings. And finally silence.

We sat it out. When it was over Anne Browder laughed in a nervous kind of way. Joe Rykler did a little soft cussing. Lew Burgoyne said, "God damn it, it ain't decent! Afore Jack ever lays a hand on that little ole girl he ought

14

to pack up her mouth with a towel. And there ain't no woman in the world ever enjoyed it that much. She's just bragging on him. I wisht to Christ they'd move off someplace into a shack in the middle of a piney woods."

"The guy it's toughest on is Rigsby," Joe Rykler said. "It about kills him to hear the proof that somebody else is getting something he can't—"

"Now, Joe," Anne Browder said.

"Am I saying something out of line?" he protested.

Alice cleared her throat. "I'll tell you all one thing. Jack Engly is a big, sweet, shy guy. But I've seen the way he can horse a two-hundred-pound fish onto the dock. And if he ever catches that damn Rigsby snuffling around Judy, Rigsby is going to be just as sorry about the whole thing as a man can get."

Judy's standard demonstration had taken the edge off the evening. It seemed to make people sort of restless. Joe wanted to go over to one of the joints on the beach. Christy said she was too tired. Lew wanted to go down into town and I decided I'd go along with him. In the end it was only Joe and Anne Browder who went over to the beach, taking off in that little blue Volkswagen that Anne and Amy Penworthy own jointly and call Herman. This was an unusual thing as it is the first time I can think of that Anne went off alone with any one of us, or any man for that matter.

I'd tried to line Anne up a couple of times but . . .

TWO

Joe Rykler

. . . I HAD ABOUT GIVEN UP on Anne. That's why it practically caught me off guard when I suddenly realized she was, in effect, accepting a date with me.

That was our first date, the same night Leo Rice arrived. I drove the little Volks out of the marina lot and went south on Broward, then turned left onto the approach to Beach Bridge with Anne Browder sitting demure and fragrant beside me.

"Any special place?" I asked her. I'd borrowed the Volks enough times so that I was familiar with the shift.

"Any place at all, Joe. But nothing fancy, the way I'm dressed."

She was in short shorts in a sort of nubby pink fabric, and wearing a sleeveless white blouse with her initials embroidered in pink over the pocket. One thing about D Dock, there are no anatomical secrets. When the gals in residence come back from work during the summer they waste no time changing into as little as the law allows.

Anne Browder is the newest resident of D Dock. She moved in with Amy Penworthy last December, two months after she had moved from New York to Elihu Beach. Amy's previous roommate, or houseboat mate, had gotten married and moved out. Amy works in the Elihu Beach Bank and Trust Company at the information desk. She is a jolly hearty gal of about thirty with pale brown hair, four million freckles and a sturdy figure. She originally came to Florida from Omaha to divorce a stinker named Milton. She and I have had a lot of good clean fun swapping horror stories about her Milton and my two expensive

16

marital mistakes. We both have some dandy anecdotes. I don't recall how Amy met Anne Browder, but at the time she met her, Anne had found a job in the office of a Doctor Harrison Blalock, and she was glad to move out of a furnished room onto the *Alrightee*.

It was agreed that Anne improved the scenery at the Stebbins' Marina. Her hair is dark blonde and she wears it in a perfectly suitable coronet braid. She is tallish, with a fine though unremarkable figure, but with superb, unforgettable legs—great long legs of particularly flawless texture, so perfect that they seemed to have a whole new range of little tender curvatures and ripenesses that you never notice on ordinary legs. As a confirmed voluptuary, may I merely say that they seemed to have more special places to kiss. Let me tell you those legs have walked through a lot of my frustrated dreams.

Anne arrived after I'd had the *Ampersand* tied up at D Dock for just about a year. I zeroed in on her right away and got nowhere. It wasn't a case of not getting to first base. I couldn't even catch a ride to the ball park. I noticed one thing about her. She smiled briefly and infrequently. She had very little to say. Her every move was curiously controlled. She could make a five-second production out of lifting a cigarette or a glass to her lips. It gave her her personality such a flavor of remoteness and coldness that all other hopefuls were chilled off. But I knew it wasn't remoteness or coldness. I had seen it before. You see it in a special kind of female, the ones who are always on the borderline of hysteria. The ones with the fires well banked, but plenty hot.

I went through my gamut, like they say, from A to B. She is about twenty-six. I am thirty-one. I am big, dark-haired and look slightly unkempt at all times. This awakens the mother in them. They want to sew on buttons and cook for me. I have brown eyes and I can look very hurt. I have various lines of patter and chatter that have proved out well. Also, I am a romantic figure. I am a writer who lives and works on his boat. They are inclined to sympathize with my creative urge to write a big novel. They are saddened that I must waste my substance by writing do-it-yourself books in order to support myself and my two ex-wives.

17

I did all my tricks for Anne Browder and she looked right through me and out the other side, wistful and, damn it, bored. She used the brush like an expert. I did some spy work, trying to dig useful information out of my old pal Amy. But apparently Anne did not indulge herself in girl talk. Amy admitted she had done some prying, but all she could learn was that Anne had quit her job in the North because of some kind of emotional involvement with somebody in the same outfit. The only sop to my pride was that she wasn't dating anybody else either.

By April I was in a frenzy. She had me wringing my hands. In May I made a serious effort to get her out of my system. I stalked the public beach until I found a cute, bright little vacationing stenographer from Atlanta, and I took her on a cruise down to Marathon. That little adventure quieted me down and I was able to finish the current do-it-yourself work briskly after I got back.

And all of a sudden, with no warning, here was Anne, legs and all, in the seat beside me. I turned north along the beach, having decided on a place called Melody Beach, where the booths are deep and dark and there is a live trio on Fridays and Saturdays, soft music in a romantic mood. It was ten o'clock and the place was half full when we went in. When those legs went by, male heads snapped around.

We got a booth. The waiter lit our candle. We decided we'd done all that could be done about beer, and so we switched, me to an Irish mist and the lady to a light rum on the rocks, with lemon twist, please.

I looked across at her. "Well!" I said. And there's a great line. It has sparkle. Somehow she could give me stage fright, make me feel as if I were sixteen again, in a rented tux.

"It's pleasant here," she said.

"Let's set up a schedule. I'm misspending my middle years. I know fun places all the way up and down the coast. I'll make out a list for us."

"Thanks, but I don't really like to go out very much, Joe."

Our drinks came. I tried to be charming. I got a few smiles, meager and polite. So I said to myself, the hell with it, and I grabbed her hand. She tried to pull it away.

18

She couldn't get it back without making a scene she apparently didn't want to make, so she let her hand rest flaccid in mine and looked at me with great coolness.

"Please let me go."

"First you listen, Anne Browder. Who are you? What are you? I want to know. Girl inside a wall a mile high. Me with no ladder. You're hurting about something. That's obvious. You need to spill it. I listen just fine. And I don't tell what I hear. Somebody clobbered you. So you're scared of everybody. I'm a harmless type. Just old Joe Rykler, friend of the working girl."

She didn't answer me. I released her hand cautiously. She yanked it back, hoisted her glass and drained it in one gulp. It was the first hasty careless motion I had seen her make. It was encouraging.

"What do you want from me?"

"I guess I want to be your friend."

"Joe! Do me the courtesy of being honest."

I leaned back. "All right. I want to hustle you into the sack. Is that a criminal urge?"

"What good would that do?"

"My God, I don't know! Does it have to be constructive? What harm would it do?"

She was looking at me intently. She moistened her lips. "It's all so pointless. It's—a compulsion."

"Who clobbered you?"

"May I have another drink, please? I clobbered myself, Joe. You see, I thought it would be a very shrewd idea to become pregnant. So he would leave his horrible wife. But when I told him, he was terrified. It turned out she was also pregnant, about four months. He hadn't mentioned it. Suddenly he was a scared little man, no longer my hero. A three-year affair ended right there, Joe, in our little hideaway full of the treasures we'd both bought for it. He knew a man who knew a man. Very reliable. It was done in Philadelphia, and they had a room where, afterward, I rested all day, counting the bricks in the wall opposite my window. I imagine the . . . result of love was given over to the municipal sewage system. They say it's very efficient."

Then the calm, cool, lovely face broke into a dozen pieces. She put her head down on the table in the crook

19

of her arm. I wondered how long it had been since she had cried. She didn't make much noise crying. Once in a while I could hear her over the music. They were playing "Lullaby of Birdland." Tears make it a sad tune indeed. I went around to her side of the booth. She didn't shrug off the arm I put around her, so I left it there. The new drinks came.

Finally she sat up, dug Kleenex out of her straw purse, dabbed at her eyes with it and honked into it. Pink and puffy around the eyes, but still lovely. I took my arm away. It was indicated.

"Joe?"

"Yes, honey."

"Joe, I can't get over it. Ten months now. I'm no nearer being over it."

"You'll have to give it more time."

"I don't love that scared little man. I loved the man I spent the three years with. I still love him."

"Love is one of the big words."

"I knew I was waiting for one man. When I met him I knew he was the one. He was the first. And maybe the last. I don't know. I'm scared."

"What should you be scared of, Annie?"

She gulped her drink again, then laid ice cold fingers on my bare forearm. "Scared of telling you the reason why I came over here with you, Joe."

"There's nothing scarey about me."

She looked at me with a discomfiting intensity, her head slightly tilted to one side, her eyes ten inches from mine. "Last May you went away for a week with that cute little girl."

"That seems to be one of the worst-kept secrets of our age."

"Why did you go away with her?"

"You mean in addition to the obvious reason? Because you, Miss Browder, had gotten under my skin. You were making me nervous. I took her like a cure."

She frowned at me. "But what about the girl, Joe? Suppose she had taken it seriously. Suppose it hurt her?"

"I didn't want that to happen. That was a problem of selection. Francie was a nice kid. She had other plans for herself. They didn't include me."

She bit her lip for a moment and then said, "So it was without love."

"When you net them by telling them you love them, it's the worst kind of cheating, Anne. Almost any man can get away with that."

"If it was without love, wasn't it . . . sort of messy?"

"Messy? I don't dig you, doll."

"Oh, just sort of coarse and greedy and empty."

"I didn't notice it was. Hell, it was fun. We provisioned the boat in Marathon and I went a way north into the islands, hundreds of them. We fished and told corny jokes and went skinny dipping over the side by sunlight and moonlight, got tan all over, ate like pigs and made love whenever it seemed like a good idea. There was no talk of love and eternity."

"I wondered if you did that because of me. I had to ask. But, Joe, how did it make you feel?"

"Relaxed. It took the tensions out. Francie was a dandy girl."

"Joe?" She looked down and drew a small slow pattern on the back of my hand with the tip of her finger. "Joe, suppose I'd gone with you instead of that Francie."

"Wait until my heart drops back out of my throat. If you'd been the one, it would have been the same only more so. A hell of a lot more so. I mean it would be like the man says—accepting no substitute."

"Get me another drink, Joe."

I signaled the waiter. I expected red welts to pop up on the back of my hand where she had drawn her shy little design.

"Anne. Anne. Do you mean what I think you mean?"

"I wouldn't want it to mean anything to you, Joe. That wouldn't be fair, because it wouldn't mean anything to me. You understand it wouldn't mean anything to me. It would be like pretend. But I wouldn't want it to be messy. I couldn't stand that. Or a stranger. It has to be somebody I like. I want it to . . . change what I am, just a little. To put . . . that brick wall further away from me. Further back. You know? I could see the edge of a window. Thirty-one bricks down that edge. In the office we had to be very remote with each other. They frowned on that sort of thing. It was a big legal office, as hushed

21

as a church. Dark suits and white blouses and not too much makeup, and no costume jewelry. They preferred pearls. But in our place I could wait, my hair tousled, musky with perfume, pacing and waiting. He could manage one night a week in the city, sometimes two. I bought one thing for us that I keep thinking about. A little Japanese shadow box, only so big, with a glass front and a place for a little light. It was a garden, a man standing with arms folded, a woman on her knees before him. Symbolic of us, I thought. When I closed the apartment I put it on the bathroom floor and smashed it to bits. The head broke off the little kneeling woman. Joe, I'm going to cry again."

"Don't. Please don't."

"Be good to me. Be gentle and careful. Is that an asinine thing to say?"

"No. No, darling."

"He got so mean and scared and nervous. He turned into a *little* man. You must understand this, Joe. There isn't any excitement in me about this. Just a sort of . . . dread. When I was little, an aunt brought me up and she had a thing about castor oil. Don't be hurt, Joe. I had to hold it a long time before I could make myself drink it. They would put it in orange juice, prune juice. Nothing helped. There isn't any wanting in me, Joe. Every day I wish I was dead." She picked up her glass.

"Keep knocking them off like that, and you are going to go out like a light."

"I can't feel them at all. You won't talk about me, Joe, to anybody?"

"For God's sake!"

"All right, but that's part of it. Being sure of that. This is such a crazy thing."

"When did you start thinking about it?"

"A month ago, I guess. Trying to be cold about it, not be a coward. Thinking if it should be Orbie or Lew or Rex or you. It came out you because you're the only one I can explain it to, really."

For months she won't talk at all, and then she hauls you into the damndest dialogue since the Greeks. I was voted the most palatable brand of orange juice. But she was drilling a nerve.

And suddenly I heard myself saying, "Maybe it isn't a smart thing for you to do, Anne. Really." I would make a nifty bandit. I'd keep slamming the safe door on my own hand.

She looked at me for three or four thousand years and said, "You couldn't have said anything better to me. Now I know I'm right."

I took her hand. It was still icy. Nervousness. "Then, to coin a phrase, honey, I'm your boy. I realize that you're asking me an enormous favor. But I'll do almost anything for my friends."

For the first time I saw more than a careful smile. It was a grin, practically, that squinched her eyes and wrinkled the princess nose, but was a little lopsided. "Keep making jokes," she said. "Make it light and unimportant. As if I were Francie." The grin went away and her eyes looked shadowy. "But don't be too hurt if . . . I find out I just . . . can't. Forgive me, if that happens. And if I can, I may be—no good"

"So we've made an executive decision on the policy level. The next step is to appoint a ways and means committee to handle the practical aspects of this matter, Miss Browder. Let's throw the peanuts on the floor and get these monkeys down off the walls."

She looked down at her fist, clenched and resting on the edge of the booth table. Her lashes were long. I had to lean a little closer to her to hear her say, "—don't want to wait and feel nervous and self-conscious. I thought the drinks would help a little."

"Pardon my crudeness, lady, but are we thinking in terms of a motel?"

Her eyes went wide. "Oh, no! I thought—your boat—"

So I overtipped a waiter enough to visibly startle him and walked out with her, following her out. Once upon a time, in Mexico with Wife One, we sat at an outdoor table and drank dark beer and I bought a lottery ticket. I bought a paper the next day and checked my number. I had to look at it at least five times before I could comprehend that I had really and truly won ten thousand pesos. With much the same feeling of incredulity combined with exaltation, I walked behind those lithe legs, behind the rhythmic clench of the pink shorts. Something, of

23

course, would happen. Some clown would bash into the Volks. Or my boat would have sunk at her mooring. Or I would get the blind staggers and fall off the dock.

D Dock was asleep. Even Sid Stark's big Chris was dark. Sid, in a prolonged evasion of civil actions in Jersey and California, lives aboard the *Pieces of Seven* with crew, tame clowns and sycophants and a busty starlet named Francesca Portoni. He throws parties for odd theatrical-looking types. Late, late parties. But the *Pieces of Seven* was dark tonight.

We walked quiet as thieves. She whispered she would be back in a little while. Amy's normal sleep is more like a coma. I went aboard my *Ampersand* and became furiously busy trying to make it look less like a hall closet. I grabbed armfuls of clutter and stowed them in random places. I stripped the bunk and remade it with fresh sheets. I turned on the quiet little fan in the forward cabin. The corner light seemed too damn bright. After a few minutes of experimentation, I found that draping it with an orange hand towel made the proper effect. I fingered the day's stubble and wondered if I should try to get in a quick shave. I wished I had champagne on ice. Cold beer didn't seem suitable. I decided she wasn't going to come back. I needed a haircut. I wondered if I ought to put pajamas on. I felt like a bride. She wasn't going to come back.

Just as I plumped the pillow for the third useless time, I felt the slight shift of the boat as she came aboard. In hurrying to meet her I managed to nearly fracture my thigh on the edge of the table across from the galley.

She came in and looked at me solemnly in the dim, dim light. She wore a hip-length pale blue terry robe, belted so tightly around the slenderness of her high waist that it flared out around the tender circle of her hips. I sensed that the only thing under that robe was Anne, and I knew she had done that deliberately, to make it that much more difficult for her to change her mind. Her eyes were huge.

"Did Amy wake—"

"Don't talk. Please," she whispered.

I led her forward to the tiny sleeping cabin. Even in my altered light, the bunk with the top sheet turned neatly down looked far too crass and methodical. So I grabbed her with great clumsiness to keep her from staring at the bunk. Noses and knees got in the way. It was as deft as a first dancing lesson. When I found her mouth, her lips were firm and cool, and I felt her tremble. I continued the nothing-kiss, wondering what the hell to do next, until she pushed me away. With frozen face and desperate bravado, and the haste of panic, she slipped the robe off and threw it aside. She stood for a bold moment, not looking at me. The perfection of her stopped my breath. Ice maiden, with a pearly translucence, so immediate she seemed unreal. Sacrificial. I realized I was feeling humble, and it seemed like a brand new emotion.

She turned the sheet further down and sat on the bunk and, still not looking at me, she lifted her arms and undid the coronet braid. Her breasts lifted with her arms. She sat with knees and ankles primly together. When her hair was undone she combed it with her fingers until it fell long and gleaming to her shoulders. She bent over and slipped her sandals off. Only then did she straighten up and look directly at me. Her mouth was trembling, her eyes uneasy, her face waxy-pale.

A most curious analogy slipped across the surface of my mind. The timid little bull finds itself in the arena and looks forlornly at the men with their pics and banderillas and the sword that kills—and the little bull knows that despite its tremblings this is what all the imitators of Hemingway call the moment of truth and it must comport itself with bravery.

"The light," she whispered. I turned it out.

We were there together possibly two hours. I tried. God knows I tried. And she did too. I am sure of that. But when she shuddered in my arms I knew it was neither excitement nor passion, but rather the reflexive tremor of the sacrificial animal. Though she tried to pretend, I could sense the regret, the remorse, the quiet despair—and the consciousness of shame. And when her breathing was rapid, it was merely the result of effort. Her rhythms had that erratic imbalance of contrivance rather than need. And when finally, in an admission of defeat, I went on to my own completion, it was but a sour spasm, lonely, meaningless and unshared. We lay deadened in the empty darkness until she gave a great sigh and climbed over me and found her robe and put it on. I got up and pulled my Bermuda Walking Shorts on, and turned on the light. Even muted, it was far too bright. We avoided each others' eyes.

We walked aft to the dark cockpit. With a special irony the skies showed twice as many stars as usual.

She touched my arm and whispered, "I'm sorry, Joe. I'm terribly sorry." And she didn't have to explain what she was sorry about.

"If at first," I said, "you don't—"

"No, Joe. That's no good. I learned something about myself. And found another dead end."

With an effort of character, I avoided the obvious pun. "A cruise is great for the inhibitions, Annie."

"It would be the same," she said hopelessly. "I guess, for me, there has to be love. And if there was, that would make it meaningful, and that isn't what I want." Her whispery voice tightened. "I wish to God I could be trivial."

She stepped on the transom and up onto the dock. We whispered good-night. I watched her walk along the dock, disappearing into shadows and then reappearing briefly under the pale dock light on its high gooseneck stanchion fifty feet away, walking in a weary way, her head slightly bowed, a night wind touching her fair hair.

And my heart burst. The tired old Rykler heart. Burst and sprayed acid into my eyes, misting the stars. I wanted to spend the next thousand years with her. So I tried to cope with the unexpected, unwanted invasion of Cupid. The little winged bastard had given up his bow and arrow and snuck up on me with a bazooka.

So I opened a beer and lit a cigarette and sat in my rickety fighting chair under the stars and talked sense to myself. You are a very cynical fellow, Rykler. You bear the wounds of two horrible marriages. That is a nice leggy blondie and you had the acquisitive urge to roll her over in the clover, and you did. Mission accomplished. End of incident. Love is a word on greeting cards. Love is not for you, Joseph. Eternity is a dirty word. She probably leaves hair in the sink, burns the toast and has a loose filling.

She is glorious. She is what it is all about.

She doesn't want an involvement any more than you do,

26

boy. And tonight proved you are not her plate of crumpets. She did everything but yawn.

I sat there. Sleep was impossible. After a while, I don't know how long, the eastern sky began to look as though Bimini was on fire. A red sun came up and turned from rose to gold. I went below. Fragrances of her were caught in my pillow, and I buried my silly nose in the pillow and felt a great sad joy.

I was hooked again, this time worse than ever before.

This time made the other times seem like the difference between a full orchestra and a penny whistle. I was on the edge of both tears and laughter.

I heard the gutsy blast of heavy marine engines and knew it was Lew Burgoyne going out on charter in the *Amberjack III.* He likes to rev them up for a long sleep-shattering minute before taking off. Crazy, black-bearded pirate. But if he is anything he is a . . .

THREE

Captain Lew Burgoyne

. . . DAMN GOOD FISHERMAN, even if I say so myself.
But too stupid to be fishing commercial the way I should
be. It's dull hard work. No laughs in it.

I guess I was looking for laughs when I took Leo Rice
on. Funny damn thing. It happened last Tuesday. Rice
had come in on Friday in that crappy Higgins. Kept to
himself. Didn't try to buddy up to anybody. We get tourists coming in here who think just because they own a
boat they can come barging right into a group of us like
old friends. So we give them the chill.

Anyway, I had a charter last Tuesday and Ron Lamarr
was going to crew for me and he didn't show up. I should
know better than to depend on that crazy kid. Anyhow, I
was outside the men's shower room bitching to Billy Looby
about having no help. This Rice was in the shower room
and I guess he heard me through the window. He came
out and said he'd be willing to help if I could use him.

I looked him over. He seemed to be in good shape.

"What do you know about it?" I asked him.

"Absolutely nothing," he said, staring me in the eye.
"If you explain what I have to do, I'll try to do it. It's
a chance for me to learn more about handling a boat."

I looked at him and I wanted to laugh out loud. This
was the same type joker who gave me such a hell of a
rough ride in the Navy. Gold on their damn sleeves. Looking at you like you were some kind of new animal. Hated
the bastards, every one.

"You last a whole day and you get a buck an hour,
Rice."

"You don't have to pay me."

"If I pay you, you're working for me. I'll pay you. See you over on the boat in two minutes, buddy."

The charter was four guys from a supermarket convention. Rice was purely a mess around a boat. I was yelling at him before we got clear of the dock. He didn't even know how to cast off a line.

On the run out to the edge of the stream I set the pilot and went back and taught him how to rig tackle and sew bait. He was all thumbs. We got into a mess of dolphin. Those supermarket boys were tougher than they looked. And they weren't feeling any pain. They yelled and whooped, and most of the time for maybe four hours we had two on at once. I worked the rear end right off that Leo Rice. I wanted to see him quit. There was something about his eyes, something uneasy, that made me think he'd quit. And about the set of his mouth.

He chopped his hands to hamburg on the raw ends of the leader wire he didn't break off right. He busted his back and blistered his hands gaffing big angry dolphin and releasing them. He untangled snarls and sewed bait and opened beer while the sun burned him and the chop bounced him around and the sweat ran into his eyes. In mid-afternoon the chop got worse and two of the supermarket guys got sick and only one made it to the rail, so that was a mop job for Rice. They wanted to come in so I brought them in. Soon as they paid off and left, I had Rice wash the boat down, and then I showed him how to rinse and lubricate the gear and stow the tackle.

When he finished I figured the time on him, and handed him eight bucks. He hesitated and then took it in his chopped-up shaky hands. He looked grayish under his tan and he stood on the dock sort of bent over a little.

"Once was enough, hey?" I said.

He looked at the boat and then he straightened up all the way and said, "Will you need help tomorrow, Captain?"

I had a half-day charter for the morning and I hadn't contacted Ron yet. If Rice was asking to be busted down, I was his man.

"Show up at seven, buddy."

He nodded and shuffled off. I figured him for too pooped to eat. He'd fall in the sack fast.

29

Rice was one of the sorriest looking things you'd ever want to see when he showed up at seven. You could tell the way he moved he was stiff all over. The charter showed up. Damn nice kids. A little Mexican couple with honeymoon written all over them.

I moved over to the gas dock and topped off the tanks. Rice handled the hose as if he was a hundred and three. But on the way out, without being told, he broke out the tackle and went to work on the bait. The sun limbered him up, but he wasn't what you'd call spry.

It was one of those perfect days. There were good fish and they were spaced right and they jumped and sparkled in the sun. The little bride got a fair sail and handled it pretty well, considering her size. I went back to grab the bill and club it. The little gal put up a yell about releasing it, not hitting it. I decided I could hold it half over the transom while Rice worked the hook out. But when he tugged at the hook that sail gave one final explosion. It wrenched the bill out of my hand and fell back into the water. The bill cracked Rice across the wrist.

By the time we got in, his wrist was swole up pretty good, but he wanted to scrub the boat down again. He was so eager I kept him around half the afternoon doing maintenance work until his tail was dragging.

I finally paid him off and said, "I got a charter tomorrow, buddy."

"Seven o'clock?"

"Right."

He showed again. I don't know what he was trying to prove. He was damn near dead on his feet, but he was beginning to be worth almost the dollar an hour I was paying him.

This charter was full day, three big-talking hardware merchants from Indianapolis. They wanted to use their own fancy equipment, drink all the bourbon they brought aboard, and catch every damn fish in the ocean.

We hit a gusty, shifty wind out of the northeast, and it built up a good chop. I could see it working on the boys. Their jokes weren't funny and they worked too hard laughing. At about eleven the fattest one tied into a mako, which is one hell of an athletic shark. Fatty was doing a poor job of handling it. Suddenly one of his pals gave up and began to unload the bourbon. That set the other one off.

And then fatty got into the spirit of things. He fumbled his way out of the fighting chair, letting the line go slack as he took the rod butt out of the socket. He made a feeble effort to hand the rod to Rice. But before Rice could grab it, the mako hit the end of the slack. Three hundred bucks worth of tackle jumped out of fatty's slack hand, bounced once on top of the fish box and took off astern.

When the boys could talk again, they let it be known they'd had it. So I turned back in. When we were in calmer water, fatty gave me the old line. We're only getting a half a day so we'll only pay for half a day. I told him the contract was for a full day and he'd pay for a full day.

"Okay," he said in a nasty way. "If that's the way you operate, here's the way I operate. I want payment for my rod and reel. I handed it to this clown you got working for you and he dropped it over the side. Right, boys?"

One of them had the decency to say, "Oh, for Chrissake, Chuck! Forget it."

"Forget, hell!" fatty yelled. He turned on Rice. "I handed it to you and you dropped it, you damn clown."

Rice stared at him a moment. Then his chin came up and his eyes seemed to darken and there wasn't anything uncertain about his mouth. He put his nose six inches from fatty's. His voice wasn't loud, but it had a lot of snap to it. "I'm no clown, you fat farce. Maybe you'd like to follow the rod you threw over."

Fatty backed away from him and said, loudly, to me, "You can't let him talk to me like this!"

"He's doing just fine," I said. I knew I'd collect in full, and I did.

For a reward I let Rice back her into the slip. I stood at his elbow giving him instructions. He let it get away from him a little and he nudged Dink Western's *Bally-Hey*. No harm done. Little smudge on the paint. He did the rest of it nice.

I paid him off and told him I didn't have a charter for Friday. That night I went over onto D Dock where the usual bunch were sitting around drinking beer. Orbie was telling what a rough day he'd had with his harem. I chipped a buck into the beer fund and took out a cold can. When I got a chance I told them about Rice, and how I hadn't been able to make him quit and how it didn't look as if I was going to. And I told them about the way he chewed the fat guy out.

Just as I finished Leo Rice came walking out along the dock toward his boat. He wore a sport shirt and slacks and I figured he'd been over on the boulevard to eat.

He nodded as he went by. When he was twenty feet beyond us I said, "Hey, Rice!"

He stopped and turned around. "Yes, Captain?"

"The name is Lew. Come on back and draw yourself a cold can of beer."

He hesitated and then came back. "Thanks," he said. He fished out the can, found the opener tied to the tub handle and opened it. The others were a little quiet and I wondered if I'd moved too fast. Hell, somebody on D Dock should have invited him first. But it was done. I hoped he'd have sense enough to drink his beer and move along. I introduced him to the others. Nobody asked him to sit down.

Just as he was finishing the can, Dink Western came swaggering out. He knows damn well he isn't welcome on D Dock. Whenever you take a close look at a bunch of charterboats, you'll find one slob. Dink was our little burden. He owns and operates the *Bally-Hey* with an ex-con mate named Dave Harran who is nice enough, but who has been ground down flat by Dink. Dink is all belly and mouth, a brawler, a guy with a mean temper. And lately he's been playing around with the young wife Captain Jimmy Meirs brought back from Georgia three months ago when old Jimmy went up there to bury his brother. Jimmy and his big black-haired bride Jannifer Jean live in a trailer back of the marina office. When Captain Jimmy is out on charter on his recently renamed *Jimmy-Jan,* it leaves Jannifer Jean, or, like Joe Rykler calls her, Moonbeam McSwine, alone. Dave Harran lives aboard the *Bally-Hey*. Dink lives ashore with his brother who is a local cop. Dink gets his business by giving kickbacks on the charter rate and by taking charters the rest of us won't touch. He runs a dirty boat.

"What you want here? What's on your mind?" Orbie

32

asked in that soft way he uses when he smells trouble.

"Nothing with you, Derr," Dink Western said. He looked at me. "Captain Jimmy says you thumped into my boat coming in."

"If I'd sunk it the basin would look prettier," I said.

"He said you had a tourist running it, Lew."

"It's all mine, free and clear, Dink. I'll let a red squirrel handle it if I feel like it."

Dink ignored me and stared at Rice. "You the one bumped me?"

"Not hard enough to do any damage," Rice said quietly.

Dink eased over to him. "I'm the one to decide about damage, pal. Any time you're within a hundred feet of my boat in any kind of boat, you keep your damn hands off the wheel no matter who tells you what to do. Got that?"

Dink had his fists on his hips.

Alice Stebbins said, "Get back where you belong, Dink."

"Ease off," Orbie said.

"Nobody bashes my boat," Dink said. He was half loaded, as usual.

Rice shrugged and turned away. Dink, in a brawler's practiced motion, grabbed Rice's arm and spun him back and hit him in the mouth. Rice sprawled on the dock. The girls squealed.

Rice stared for a moment, blood on his chin, and then got up fast. You could tell in ten seconds he didn't have a chance in the world against Dink, but when a man chooses to fight, you let him have it to himself. I think he got knocked down four times in return for getting in one pretty good lick. He was awful slow getting up onto his hands and knees after the fourth time. The girls were screaming to have it stopped. I was curious as to just how many times he would get up. I had the feeling that so long as he was conscious, he'd keep trying.

But as he was trying to come up from his hands and knees the fourth time, Dink took one step forward and kicked Rice so hard in the pit of the stomach he lifted him clean off the dock, maybe six inches in the air.

And then I knew it was time. Orbie had the same yen. We'd both been waiting for the right chance. We got up at the same time.

Alice knew what was up right away. "Not on the

dock!" she yelled. "Not on the dock!"

As Dink stared at us, Orbie slapped a coin onto the back of his hand and said to me, "Call it right for first."

"Tails," I said.

"You're wrong," Orbie said. He grinned at Dink and hit him a clean shot under the eye without warning, and turned and ran like a rabbit. Dink roared and lumbered after him. As soon as Orbie was on shore he turned and squared off. It was a good quick way to get Dink off the dock.

It drew a pretty good crowd. All men except for Jannifer Jean, Alice and Judy Engly. Their faces had a raw, hungry look. There was enough to look at.

It went maybe forty minutes, or twice that long, or half that long. It's hard to tell, watching a fight like that. They fought under the light thirty feet from the shore end of D Dock, toward charterboat row. Orbie was fast like I expected, but Dink had a right like a sledge. Three times Orbie went down and had to scramble out of range fast when Dink came in to stomp him.

And then it began to go Orbie's way. He was giving away thirty pounds or more, but he was in better shape. He hooked Dink in the belly until he got the arms down, and then he shifted to the head. I could tell when he started to try to finish him off, but he couldn't knock Dink off his feet. He could stagger him, but he couldn't put him down.

Finally Dink staggered back until he was leaning against the skinny lamp post, able only to make slow pawing motions with his hands. Orbie was gasping. It was quiet. You could hear the smack of fist on flesh in slow cadence. We stood in a circle in the night, sucking in our wind with each chunk.

Dink's knees buckled but he struggled back up. You didn't hear anybody yelling to stop it. Dink isn't a popular man.

When Orbie finally paused, arm weary, I stepped out and said, "You ain't leaving me so damn much, Orbie."

"Take your shot," he gasped.

Dink stared at me stupidly. I grabbed his shirt, swung him away from the pole and hit him three times. The last time was while he was on his way down. He landed on his face. I heard the long sigh from the people watching. My hands stung.

Dink grunted, rolled over and sat up slowly, bloody mouth agape. I sat on my heels beside him and said, "Get up, Dink."

"No," he said in a faraway rumble.

"This the first time you been down, boy. You got to get up one time anyhow."

He shook his massive head. "Stayin' right here. You kin stomp me, you want to. But I won't get up."

"Git up!" Jannifer Jean yelled.

He shook his head. Orbie and me, we walked back out onto D Dock, leaving him there with people staring at him, and some of them had begun to laugh. Dink had been due a long time. He got off easy. In the old days down in the Keys somebody would have run a shark hook up through his jaw and used braided cable to tow him across the oyster bars and coral until the hook came loose.

The group had shrunk. It was down to Joe, Gus, Anne and Amy. We opened new beers and then stepped aboard the *Mine* to check damage. The whole left side of Orbie's face had begun to puff out, closing his eye. And on both hands he had dimples where his knuckles had been.

"You're a sorry mess," I told him.

"I feel just fine, Lew. Just fine. Sorry I didn't leave you much."

"The little I had was right nice, thanks."

We went back onto the dock. "Where'd Rico go?" Orbie asked.

Anne answered. "Christy helped him back to his boat right after you took off. She hasn't come back yet."

"Is a nice fella," Gus said firmly. And that was the decision. If Rice wanted to join the group, he was in. I hadn't moved too fast, but Dink had helped me prove it. But I still couldn't figure Rice out. He didn't fit any of the slots you put people in.

Amy said, "I guess Christy has always had a suppressed desire . . ."

FOUR

Christy Yale

. . . TO BE A NURSE, when I was a little kid. I remember one Christmas they gave me a toy nurse kit, stethoscope and all. But somehow I never even gave it a try. Now I'm Miss Christine Yale, Girl Friday of the Elihu Beach Chamber of Commerce.

I was in the forward cabin of Rice's *Ruthless,* sitting on the unused bunk looking at Leo Rice in the other bunk, propped up on a pair of pillows, a dark strong highball in his hand.

"Feel better?" I asked.

"Ask me when I've gotten this drink down. They introduced us but . . . I'm sorry . . . I don't quite . . ."

"Christy. Christy Yale."

His smile was slow and pleasant. "Christy Yale, Samaritan."

"It was a pretty stinky introduction to our little group, Leo."

"Who broke it up?"

"They should have broken it up right away, but they had to wait until he kicked you, darn them."

"Oh, he only kicked me. I had the feeling he dropped a cruiser on me."

"Orbie and Lew broke it up. They took him ashore. By now they've had a chance to beat him half to death. I think they've been waiting for a good opening. He's an impossible man."

"Improbable is a better word. I don't remember ever running into that type before—at least so intimately."

"It seemed especially awful, Leo, because—because you're just not the sort of man that happens to."

"What do you mean by that?"

"You have a sort of manner of importance about you, no matter how you're dressed. A sort of dignity. I don't know how to say it. A gentleman, I guess."

"You make me sound like a horrible stuffed shirt."

"Oh, you're not!"

He chuckled and it made him grimace with pain. "How would you know whether I am or not, Christy?"

"Am I blushing? Leo, who are you? What do you do?"

"Well . . ."

"Understand that questions are not good form around here. But I'm an incurable snoop."

"The answer is pretty ordinary, Christy. I'm a corporation executive from Syracuse, New York. I got very run down—for many reasons. So I took a six-month leave of absence."

"You didn't look so run down when you arrived."

"I got into the car and drove. You should have seen me. Thirty pounds heavier. Flabby, jittery. I ended up in Jacksonville. I rented an isolated beach cottage and I bought a shovel."

"A shovel!"

"To improve my health and character. Every day I shoveled beach sand from here to there, and the next day I would shovel it all back. More every day. Finally I found myself admiring myself in the mirror, flexing muscles and so on. So I sold the car and bought a boat. I wanted to be a valiant mariner. Calm in the eye of the tempest, steely hand at the helm."

I saw the obvious chance to trap him. "Why did you stop here, Leo?"

"I had the vague idea of going down to the Keys, but I found that boats make me nervous. I keep worrying about going aground, and what the markers mean, and what to do about other water traffic, and what part of the boat is going to suddenly stop operating."

"So you stopped right here?"

"To get my wind."

"I'm a horrible snoop, Leo. I told you that."

There was a sudden wariness about him. "Yes?"

"You got here last Friday. There was a letter in the box in the office for you on Saturday. From Syracuse, from a law firm I think. Addressed to you, care of Stebbins' Marina, aboard the *Ruthless*. So you meant to come here."

"I laid out a route," he said, too casually.

"Don't spoil it. I love intrigue," I said.

"And what would be my mysterious mission?" he asked lightly but guardedly.

I put my chin on my fist and scowled at him. "I suppose Sid Stark would be the most logical. He's in all sorts of tax trouble. Maybe you're a sort of undercover agent, finding out how much he's spending on all those parties."

"Hmmm. Any other ideas?"

"Well, you could be working for the syndicate which has been trying to buy this place from Alice and turn it into an expensive and mechanized yachtsman's paradise. Then all we common people will have to move out."

"Miss Yale, you have a lurid imagination."

I liked looking at him and talking to him. His hands were good, lean, strong and long-fingered. I have a thing about hands. And it was an ugly-nice face, not improved by the bulging purple bruise on the right cheekbone, the puffed lips and the split on the side of chin, iodined and bandaged by me. On a man that kind of a face is fine. I can tell you what it does to you if you are of the female persuasion and have a Halloween face.

"You're married, aren't you?" I blurted. I have a nasty knack of not knowing what I'm going to say until I hear myself say it. In the past this has created quite a few problems down at the good old C of C.

"I was married, Miss Christy. I married young. My wife is dead. I've got two kids in boarding school, two boys, fifteen and sixteen. They're in summer camp now."

"Pry, pry, pry," I said.

"Why were you so positive about me being married? It's happened before. I've always wondered."

I tried to figure out why I'd been so certain. "I suppose it's a certain . . . aura of unavailability, Leo. Maybe a sort of naturalness in the company of a woman. As if you don't have to prove anything. A woman senses the absence of the wolf call. Fix us some fresh things?"

He looked at his empty glass and then held it out. "Shank of the evening, but please make mine look less like iced coffee without cream this time."

When I came back from the little galley with the two drinks he looked at me with evident curiosity. "While you were gone, Christy, I realized what's been bothering me about you, on practically a subconscious level."

"Hey, now!"

"Diction. When you talk casually you get that cracker slur and twang that I'll swear is legitimate. But when you say something thoughtful, like telling me why I look married, you speak with a certain amount of precision."

"That calls for the story of my life, stranger. Lay back. My pappy and all us Yales were born right here. Of course, looking at the town now, it's like saying you were born on a merry-go-round at a carnival. But it wasn't like this when I was a little kid. It was quiet and nice. No neon and floodlights and swimming pools and horrible glass jalousies.

"Born here twenty-nine years ago, to be desperately accurate, stranger. Me and my four brothers. They're all older, all very conservative, all married. They're scattered up and down the coast, disapproving violently of their little sister living on a houseboat in a junky marina. Disgraceful bohemianism. Mother was a doll, and Daddy sure wanted a Southern-type belle in the family. It confused him when I began to look like Mickey Rooney, from the neck up. But I did have a lovely voice. He decided if I couldn't have looks, I could have brains, so I was the only Yale he sent North to school.

"First year in boarding school I was playing a lady-like game of field hockey and a girl who looked like Tony Galento whaled me across the throat with her stick. I whispered for three months and when my voice came back, it came back like this. Like a boy with laryngitis at the time his voice is changing. Daddy wanted to sue. I spent six years in the North. Boarding school and Smith College. I came back and rattled around a while, then found my niche in the Elihu Beach Chamber of Commerce. I live aboard the *Shifless* with Helen Hass. The name of the boat is symbolic."

"Is it a bohemian life?" he asked.

"That isn't the word. I'd say casual. You've had a taste of how casual it can get tonight. You get a chance here to . . . say what you please and do what you please.

39

There're very nice people here, Leo. You'll find that out if you stay. But I guess it's sort of a revolt against the way most people live. It can get . . . violent around here. And funny. And crazy. It's never monotonous."

"That I can believe. I haven't been hit in the face or hit anybody else for twenty years. It was very unreal. Like finding yourself in a B movie."

"It didn't work like the B movies. The hero got clobbered."

"I don't feel like the hero type. I could have done just as much damage flailing him with a paper towel."

"Leo, what's the object of crewing for Lew?" I asked him.

"Object? It's a chance to learn what they didn't have time to teach me in Jacksonville."

"But it's learning the hard way. Lew Burgoyne is rough."

"I couldn't help but notice. Christy, I'm full of platitudes. Basically I'm a very dull man. I believe if you want to pick up something fast, you put yourself in a spot where you have to learn."

"Throw the baby off the dock and yell 'Swim to Mommy, dear'?"

"Exactly."

"One word in there bothers me. Why do you have to learn fast?"

Once again I detected uneasiness and wariness in him. His smile was too casual. "Impatience, I guess."

Conversation had run out. I had the feeling that he and I could talk to each other for years, and enjoy every minute, but for the moment we had run out and I knew sleep would be good for him. Time for me to leave.

There was a little pause after I finished my drink. Not a particularly awkward pause, but I filled it with one of my faces, the one with owl eyes and a goldfish mouth. It got the familiar grunt of laughter from him. I stood up and said, "Slave girl leave king on bed of pain now."

"Christy, I'm very grateful."

" 'Night, now."

"Just a moment." He was looking at me with such a discomfiting intensity that I thought maybe there was a streak of the wolf there. "Why did you do that?"

"Do what?"

"Make that face for no reason."

"Oh, that! It's just one of my faces. I'm Christy, the clown girl. A laugh a minute. Here's one of my greatest." I put the glass down and did my ape walk, knuckles almost on the floor, and made my ape face.

He laughed and then said, "I laughed, but it made me feel uncomfortable to laugh."

I stared at him. "Why?"

"Because it's like a nervous tic. I sense something compulsive about it."

"Stranger, are you an exec or an undercover psychologist?"

"I guess I've always had to know what makes people do things, say things, form opinions."

I felt very odd. Though we'd talked quite a lot, there had been an impersonal flavor about it. And suddenly it had become very personal, very immediate. To keep people out of your secret places, you make jokes.

"Question, then, is why Christy is a compulsive clown? Because people tell me I have a nifty sense of humor and I have to live up to it."

"Is that all?"

"Well, to be a clown, you have to have the face to go with it. Then you practice. And pretty soon people are laughing like crazy. And you become a very popular girl." I'd tried to keep it light, but something worse than usual happened to my voice. And my darn eyes started to sting. "What difference does it make?" I asked belligerently.

"The last thing I want to do is make you feel bad, believe me. I was just wondering about you. I'm sorry."

"No harm done, stranger. Take care."

"Christy?"

I turned back again, warily. He had a horrible knack of making me feel exposed and uncomfortable. But I saw that he was the one looking uncomfortable. "What you said earlier, Christy, about the letter, joking about a secret mission. I'd appreciate it if you wouldn't talk to the other people about it."

"Then I *was* right!"

"In a sense. Yes."

"What are you here for?"

41

"I'll make this promise to you. If I can tell you, I will."

"Okay."

"And you're a great deal prettier than you think you are, Christy."

"Don't!" I wailed, and fled like a thief. I stumbled getting up onto the dock because he had turned the sting to tears and I wasn't seeing too well.

Some of the gang were still down there by the *Lullaby,* but I didn't want to join them. I went aboard the *Shiftless.* I was glad Helen wasn't home. It was just nine o'clock. On Thursdays she went to Spanish class and got back after ten.

You go along, minding your own business, and you get the illusion of invulnerability until somebody comes along and shows you how easy it is to peel off all your armor. Leo had brought Jerry back to me, brought him back to life. Big solemn gentle Jerry. Before Jerry there had been boys who made the automatic social gesture of trying to kiss the clown girl. I disguised terror with a buffoonery that collapsed them. Until Jerry. At first he responded to my clowning with a tolerance that was almost solicitude, as though I had a rash or a stammer. I could not divert him. And pretty soon I loved him with all my heart.

He wouldn't let me go into any of my acts or imitations, or make any of my faces when I was with him. He said I was very funny and later on I could amuse the hell out of our children, but right now he felt more comfortable being in love with a girl instead of a joke book, and for him I could, by God, be a girl-type girl. And I was. For him. Thoroughly girl.

He told me I was beautiful, and it made me feel beautiful and when I felt beautiful, I didn't have to be hilarious.

Then, with marriage inevitable, there was a little hitch in the timing. We decided to be very sensible and delay it until after his participation in a certain police action. Not a war, of course. God damn all sensibleness, all logical decisions, all reasonableness. They killed him over there, on a hill with a number instead of a name, and when they're dead you can't tell whether it was a police action or a war. So I went through all the motions of life for a year, while my heart rotted in my chest. No kids to amuse. No new name.

42

After a yea[...]
up on all my acc[...]
race. At least my [...]
the beach, twice in [...]
and so damn wonder[...]
empty nights.

So you make all the a[...]
boards, sweep out the floor [...]
indifference for the years when [...]
old woman. Then, without warning, [...]
comes into your life and responds [...] so
reminiscent of Jerry that all the tidy[...]one.
Debris all over the place. It isn't fair.

I sat in the dark for a while and then [...]ed on a
light and looked at myself in the mirror, trying to see
prettiness. I really looked. Not that half-conscious morning
inspection.

This hair—a coarse cropped thatch in four beach-
bleached shades of sand and brown. This too-round face,
devoid of any suggestion of a romantic gauntness. An after-
thought of a nose, so inconsequential as to look embryonic.
Mouth enough for a girl and a half. Eyes of a funny shade
of green under furry black brows set into a face so asym-
metrical that the left one is noticeably higher than the
right. The figure, I freely admit, is a little jim-dandy.
Things seem to be in the right places in the right quan-
tities. It is a good and faithful gadget that can water ski
all day without complaint, digest scrap iron, and slay any
virus foolhardy enough to come within range. Only Jerry
knew how well and quickly it learned its primary function.
But unused now. Aching at times from disuse. Sad faithful
gadget, whose basic remaining function is to hold this
silly head five feet four inches off the ground.

Be pretty, girl, like the man says. So I moistened my
lips and blinked my eyes at myself and attempted a provocative smile. I looked like an urchin stifling a gastric
disturbance. I knew what was coming then. First time in
years. It took me thirty seconds to strip, slip into my bed—
teeth unbrushed—and huddle into a sour little ball of
misery, with the pillow in a strategic position. I made it
just in time.

Within seconds it was upon me, and I was snorting,

...e pillow, the sobs knotting
...sty cries, she goes all the way,
...agony. When it's over, and it usually
...me, my face looks as if my head had been
...beet juice.

...ended, as it always does, and I lay spent and, in some
measure, content. With a ghost of a sob once in a while,
like a remote hiccup. Heard the night sounds. Whispery
hum of traffic. Lap of water. High whee of a jet. Music
somewhere nearby. A man laughing.

You can't hardly get good armor any more. The kind
you can get, it dents easy. And rusts in damp weather. And
the joints squeak. And if you try to chunk your lance into
a windmill, the seams split on you.

I wonder if Anne's armor is better than mine.

And what brand is Leo Rice wearing?

I have the feeling that something is ending around here.
An era. The end of a piece of my life. It's a restless feeling of change, and with a smell of violence about it. As
if the fight tonight was just a sample. I don't like fights ...

FIVE

Alice Stebbins

... BUT SOMEHOW I HAVE TO WATCH THEM, even though they make me sick to my stomach. How many have I seen here since I married Jess ten years ago? More than a dozen scary ones, like tonight. I don't count the tourist fights, when they get to scrapping about their women. They get drunk, take a few wild punches, then grab each other and roll around until they run out of wind.

I mean the man-fights, like tonight. Mike used to love a fight. He said it was a good hobby for a construction man. He'd come home all banged up and happy as a clam, win or lose. Twenty-two good years with Mike, from when I was seventeen to when I was thirty-nine. Had the one boy and lost him when he was eleven, and from then on the years weren't quite as good. But good enough. Until a cable snapped and whipped and cut him into two pieces. Even if I think of that a thousand more times, it will make my stomach turn over every time. But you could never tell it, looking at him in the coffin.

That first outfit he was with, they built a new highway across the farm. The day the job ended, when they all tossed their hats into the last slab poured, I ran off with him, so crazy in love I didn't care if he married me or not. But he did.

It's a crazy world, how a farm girl from west of Columbus can end up owning a boat yard. Always wanted to see Florida. After Mike was gone, nobody was more alone. In construction you never settle long enough in one place to put down roots.

I got permission to fish off the end of B Dock. Ten years

ago you could catch fish in the basin. Not any more. Restful to sit and fish. Jess got into the habit of wandering out every day for a little chat. It took me a while before I could understand everything he said. He would stay a little longer every day. I told him about the farm and Mike and the boy and the accident, and all the places we'd lived. He told me about working on the trawlers when he was a boy, and how his three brothers drowned in a hurricane, and how he came to buy fifteen acres of land for a boat yard. He told me about his two wives and what they died of and when, and how his son got killed in a plane crash in the early part of the war and how his daughter died of leukemia.

I remember the day I told him it was my fortieth birthday. There's this about a birthday. Even when you know it doesn't mean a thing, you feel as if you have to tell somebody. So I told him. When I was leaving late that afternoon, he called to me and asked me in, and that was when I first climbed those narrow stairs up to this apartment. He had a store-bought cake he'd gone out and gotten, with Alice written on it in green goo, and four little blue candles. Being so alone after never being alone your whole life, you get edgy. All of a sudden I couldn't stop bawling. He was walking back and forth, wringing his hands, and practically bawling himself. He'd stop every little bit and pat me on the shoulder real timid.

After I got over it the candles had burned down and out. I cooked up some fish and hash-brown potatoes and we ate, and he put new candles on the cake and I blew them out. We ate some of the cake and then talked until about midnight.

Four days later he asked me up again. He was acting solemn and nervous. He had something on his mind, but he couldn't seem to get it out. He kept telling me I was a young woman. That was a laugh. I felt as young as Grandma Moses. And then, after some fumbling, he showed me a piece of paper he'd written a list on. The old sweetie had listed his assets, the marina free and clear, government bonds and so on. He told me he was sixty-two. I found out later he was really sixty-four. I finally realized he was asking me to marry him. Thank God I neither laughed nor cried. I said I'd think it over. We were both

46

so alone. That was the worst part. Being so alone. I wondered what Mike would think if he could see me thinking about marrying Jess Stebbins, a knotty little old guy with that big ruff of white hair and those washed-out blue eyes in a face sun-dark as a saddle. I've always been a big horse. I stood eye to eye with Jess and outweighed him fifteen pounds. Mike would roar that big laugh, but he'd understand. No one should ever be completely alone.

I decided to say yes the next day, and waited three more days before telling Jess. The mayor, one of his old buddies, married us in his office in City Hall. Jess and I moved my stuff into this apartment. We had to have half a truckload of junk carried away to make room.

About the physical part of it, I didn't know what to expect. After the ceremony he kissed me quick and timid. I knew I didn't feel any more response to him than I would to your granddaddy, but if he figured that was part of the bargain, I wasn't going to hold out on him. I needn't have worried about him. By the end of the first week I had some pretty strong suspicions of what had killed off his first two wives. And my responses were all in order. I wasn't complaining a bit. After twenty-two years with a man like Mike, you build up fires that never go out. Jess loved to have me joke him about his virility, expressing awe and alarm. He'd stick his chest out and swagger up and down. After our first couple of weeks he slowed down to the pace of a sailor on leave.

It was a good three years, all but the last three months. Except in that one department, he was the laziest man alive. Anybody can see how this marina grew into a pretty fair business. It grew like a mushroom patch. Nothing matches. Everything needs paint. Everything is about to fall down.

After he took sick, it took him three months to die, and he died hard. I don't think the body weighed sixty pounds. I nursed him twenty hours a day, and slept for a week after the funeral. He left me everything, with cash for taxes.

Maybe it's the climate, or maybe it's being on the water. I don't know. I had big plans to do all the fixing up and enlarging Jess never got around to. I put it off and put it off. Now I'm as no-account as he ever was, I guess. But I have roots. And friends. And Gus Andorian.

He's a lot more like Mike than Jess was. And now that I'm fifty, Gus doesn't seem as old as Jess did when I was forty. It started between us nearly three years ago, in a damn fool way. I woke up about two one morning and thought I smelled smoke. I'm scared to death of fire around this place. I put a robe on and went down to look around. I couldn't find anything. It was a moonlit night, but I didn't see a six-inch chunk of two-by-four until I stepped on it. I twisted my ankle and fell on my face. I used some of the language I had learned from Mike as I was getting up. When I put my weight on the ankle I went down again and said some of the words I had overlooked the first time.

I'd made it on my hands and knees to within ten feet of the office door when Gus loomed up in the moonlight, full of beer and curiosity, on his way back to his old scow, the *Queen Bee*.

"What the hell are you doing?" he rumbled at me.

I told him in several dozen well chosen words. In spite of my alarmed protests, he picked up the solid hundred and fifty pounds with impressive ease and carried me upstairs. I sustained further injuries in transit. He thumped my head on one door frame and my good ankle on another.

He plumped me down on the bed so hard I bounced. He knelt and fingered the puffed ankle with great gentleness and murmured sympathy. He made me work my foot until he was satisfied I hadn't broken anything. I told him which cupboard to look in for sheeting. He tore some long strips and did a professional-looking job of binding it and tying the ends.

He knelt, admiring his handiwork, and then looked up at me. There was a sort of a click you could almost hear. And in the next second he sprang like a lion. I fought for maybe two whole seconds. Afterwards he wept, bashed his deep chest with his fist, demanding I call the police and have him locked up forever. He shouldn't be free to assault innocent ladies. Finally I got it through his thick skull that the lady didn't mind a bit. His whole craggy face turned into one vast mask of surprise.

"Yah?" he said.

"Yah."

So he came back to bed. After a few months I learned not to ask him to make an honest woman of me. I meant it, too. But much as he loved the little dictator who kept him in line for so many years, marriage is not a good word to him. He was kept on short rations, I think. He is a big kid. This is like stealing apples. It gives him a delicious feeling of guilt. When he tiptoes, carrying his shoes, he lifts his knees so high he looks like a football player in slow motion. When he goes, Ssssh, half the night drivers on the Boulevard wonder if they're getting a flat tire. He feels romantic and devilish.

I feel guilt too. And sometimes I feel ridiculous. Yet, again, we are two lonely people. Who are we hurting? But guilt is there.

I sat in the apartment by the window that looks out toward the basin. It was after ten. I saw Helen Hass walking out toward the *Shifless*. The little nightly beer picnic on D Dock had ended. Boat lights made tracks across black water.

It's a good place. I'll miss it.

The sound of the television in the little lounge just off the office came up through the floor. I knew who was down there. That damn Jannifer Jean, that swamp-pussy poor crickety old Jimmy Meirs brought back from Georgia three months ago. She's maybe twenty to his fifty, but who am I to talk? Buys pretties for her. Cooks for her. Makes a damn fool of himself. If he'd ever married before, maybe he'd be smarter. He found himself a sweet chunk of trash for sure. Probably her last chance to get out of the swamps and she grabbed it. Just about smart enough to find her mouth with a fork. And from the look of her you can just tell that she got started off at twelve or thirteen and hasn't stopped for breath since.

She hadn't been here a week before that damn Dink Western got to her while Jimmy was off on charter. About the only streak of decency in her is not taking anybody into the trailer. Maybe she knows if I caught her at that I'd throw her off the place, Jimmy or no Captain Jimmy. She can move around from bunk to bunk.

Came near throwing her off the place that day last month when she went aboard that boat over at B Dock. Those three hotshots from Miami were aboard. Went aboard in the afternoon and didn't come off until nine, with Captain Jimmy, in off his charter, about to lose his mind about her. Came off half drunk and smeary-looking and told Jimmy a batch of lies he swallowed. Next morning the boat pulled out, and that afternoon Jannifer Jean went into town and came back with a whole new batch of those tight pants and tight shirts in bright colors. So I know she hustled those Miami boys, but I don't know how she explained to Jimmy where the money came from.

Damn if I can understand men sometimes, how any one of them'd want to touch her. That long tangly black hair, and that long white face the sun won't touch, and those big dull-looking black eyes, and that big bloody-looking mouth. Maybe it's what's under those tight shirts, great huge soft white things, so big there's something disgusting about them, at least to me. She's slim enough around the middle, and then comes those pulpy hips and those long lardy legs. Those thighs have a loose quiver when she walks. And it's some walk. I won't ever forget Christy Yale staring at her one day as she walked away from us and saying, in a sort of reverent voice, "Alice, when Moonbeam walks on the level, she looks like a sack of melons rolling downstairs."

And she never looks clean. Her feet are grubby as a small boy's hands. I keep wanting to get yellow soap and a stiff brush and scrub her neck for her.

Right in front of her, Captain Jimmy said proudly to me, "Alice, don't she look exactly like Jane Russell?"

Jannifer Jean gave me a sappy smile. I swallowed hard and said, "Exactly, Jimmy." God help me.

I'm pretty certain even Rex Rigsby put her through her paces one time. I can't understand it. Rigsby certainly has no trouble finding better material. Poor Captain Jimmy. He must have heard the way Moonbeam screamed at Dink Western to get up.

So Jimmy is asleep in the trailer and she's down there now. The bad thing is that Judy Engly may be with her. Jack ought to keep Judy away from her. They've been going over to the beach together. A bad thing. Jack can make her sound like a sack of cats, but still she's acting restless. Meant to have kids.

So now I've talked myself into putting my shoes on and going down there and, if Judy is there, busting it up.

I went down the narrow stairs and into the dark office. I walked to the doorway to the little lounge and looked in. Jannifer Jean sat sloppy on the rattan couch, all alone, one white leg folded under her. She had a box of popcorn. She was chewing slowly, eyes on the screen. Every once in a while she would dip her hand in the box, shove more into her mouth, and then lick the tip of each finger.

I went in and turned the volume down to where it belonged. On the screen they were about to hang a cowboy.

"You deaf?" I asked her.

She looked at me with those dull eyes, chewing like a sleepy cow. "Lahk it loud," she said.

"Keep it turned down, hear?"

"Show thing, Miz Stebbins." She was watching the screen again.

"And lock the outside door when you leave. It was unlocked yesterday morning."

"Show."

I sighed. They hung the cowboy. I turned to go back upstairs. A voice in the dark on the other side of the screen door said, "Alice?"

"Who is it?"

"George Haley." He opened the screen door and came in.

"George, you're a damn pest."

"Hell, I know that. But something new came up."

"Come on up, then."

He followed me up to the apartment, breathing hard on the stairs. He's a big soft man with an oddly small head, a sun-red face, big black glasses and a gay wardrobe of pastel slacks and gaudy sports shirts which are always worn hanging outside the pants. His real-estate office is half a mile south on Broward, a little air-conditioned cinder block building not as big as the sign on the roof. DEAL DAILY WITH HALEY.

I opened us a pair of beers. He sat in Jess's big chair and I sat in the rocker.

"Late for a business call, George?"

"I saw the lights. Thought I'd take a chance."

I decided to needle him some. "How you coming along

51

with the most beautiful girl in Florida? Agnes thrown you out of the house yet?"

His face got redder. "Now I'm telling you, like I told Agnes and like to tell everybody that's got the wrong idea—I hired Darlene Marie Moyd for pure business reasons."

"Sure, George."

"And it's working out, too. You'd be surprised how many more customers come in the office."

"Men."

"They buy the property, Alice. And another thing. I leave that door open so she can't help hear what goes on in my office. You'd be surprised how many men, knowing a girl like that can hear, won't dicker as much as usual. It's a pure business thing with me."

"Wouldn't it look better if she could type?"

"Her typing is coming along real good. I don't know why everybody has to go around thinking I—"

"What's this new thing that came up, George?"

He looked happy to be off the subject of the winner of fourteen beauty contests. He leaned forward.

"Now you know, Alice, you've been pretty slippery about talking to the boys who want this place."

"I never said I wanted to sell. And if I did, what they offered is ridiculous."

"I've wasted time talking sweet to you. Now I'm going to put the cards right out where you can see them. This is a crummy, run-down place. It's a damn eyesore. It's hampering the development of the land around it. Important people own some of the land around it. They want to see that land value go up. You haven't got the capital to improve this place. And so, sooner or later, in one way or another, they're going to squeeze you out of it. Right?"

And I knew he was right. When they decided it was time, they could dig up enough city ordinances to close me down. Jess was always able to handle city and county commissioners, but he couldn't do me any good now.

George said, "I've kept them off your back, Alice. This has been building for a year. I want a good commission out of it. And I won't get it if I let them close you down. Right?"

52

"Keep talking."

"I admit the syndicate offer was a little low—"

"Low! It was less than the value of the land with nothing on it, George."

"Do you know why?"

"What do you mean?"

"You aren't zoned right."

"I'm zoned right for what I'm doing, George."

"But not for what they want to do. They want to tear everything out, put in new docks, shops, a motel, and a big restaurant and bar. But they couldn't be sure they could get a zoning change."

"I see."

"Today they fixed it so they know they can get the zoning change. They cut the Decklin brothers in. They're the ones could have blocked it. And they're the ones that can guarantee it will go through. So now they can go higher."

"How high?"

"Hundred and eighty thousand. Twenty down, balance in equal installments over eight years at five per cent. You hold a first mortgage."

"That isn't a lot higher."

"It's thirty thousand more, and that seems to me like a lot of money, somehow. And I'll take my commissions out of the payments as they come along instead of out of the first chunk. Okay?"

"I don't know, George. I don't know."

"Use your head, Alice. You know those Decklins. Now that they're in on it, and believe me, the boys thought a long time before letting them in—they squeeze so hard, you haven't got a prayer in hell of selling to anybody else. Nobody bucks the Decklins on this coast."

"I don't know why this has to happen, George. Why can't they leave me alone? I make enough to pay the help and support myself. Who am I hurting?"

"The city can use a first-class marina, Alice. Like down in Lauderdale."

I got up and went over to the window and looked out across the big boat basin. Something big was moving south down the waterway. Opposite the entrance to my place they started to give their three longs for the Beach Bridge.

A little while later I heard the bridge siren and I could see the flashing red of the signal that stopped traffic across the bridge.

I knew that if you took the Stebbins' Marina and stuck it way off somewhere by itself, it wouldn't be worth twelve cents. The important money was for the land, which Jess had paid six hundred dollars for a long, long time ago.

"Where will the people go, George, the ones living here?"

"What do you care about that?" he asked in an irritable way. "You responsible for them? You haven't been charging them as much as they should pay for years."

"They're my friends."

"For God's sake, Alice!"

"And where'll I go?"

"With that money you can live about any place you feel like. Do some traveling, maybe."

"How much time have I got?"

"I wouldn't say you got too much time. I've been telling them you're going to be reasonable."

"Every year, you know, they give me a surprise birthday party. You came to the last one."

"I'm not about to forget it."

"I'll let you know then, George."

"I forgot when it is."

"The thirtieth. A Saturday."

"This is only the seventh. That's a long time. I don't know if—"

I turned around from the window. I'd had enough of being pushed. "That's the way it is, George. It isn't going to be no different, no matter what you say."

"Don't get sore, Alice."

"And you got yourself something to do the rest of the month. I'm paying the commission. They're not. You go get me a better price, hear?"

"But it's—"

"Maybe some other real-estate people can get me a better price, George."

I saw him get sore and cover it up quickly. He did a little wheedling. But he knew my mind was made up. And, damn him, he knew what the answer had to be when I'd tell him on the thirtieth. I was being pushed out. It's a hell of a word they use—a marginal operation. It means you just get along. No money for fancy improvements and maintenance.

When he left, I went down with him. Moonbeam was gone. She'd put the door on lock. I let George out. The night was soft and quiet. Traffic had thinned out on Broward. Just as George started out of the lot, there was a terrible squealing and yelping of tires and I braced myself for the sound of the crash. But nothing happened. In the Boulevard lights I saw the little white Triumph turn into the lot and park. So Rex Rigsby was back. He took a suitcase out and then started to put the top up on the little car. I strolled out.

He turned and looked at me and said, his voice a little shaky, "Who was that damn fool, Alice?"

"Deal Daily with Haley."

"I was turning in. He didn't even look."

I saw no point in mentioning the fact that if George had killed him, it would have been an excuse for general rejoicing. "Rex, you took off without catching up on your rent like you promised. And you got a gas bill and a laundry bill and a repair bill."

"I was a little short."

"If that was true, I wouldn't lean on you. But I know damn well you're not short. You're just close with money, Rex. You got it and I want it."

"Now, Alice—"

"Don't turn on the charm, boy. It won't work. Don't bother smiling. Just pay up."

"First thing in the morning."

"For all I know the *Angel* will be gone in the morning and I'll sit here a couple weeks wondering if I could attach this little car. You come in the office right now, boy, and pay up."

"Can I finish putting the top up, please ma'am?"

"You can do that, yes."

He came into the office. I turned the lights on and opened the file and got his bills out, added them up. He owed a hundred eighteen seventy. He looked them over real careful, and then the son of a gun took a bill clip out of the pocket of his linen shorts, thick with money folded once. He put down two fifties and a twenty without

55

making it look any thinner. I marked the bills paid and gave him his change. He shoved it loose into his pocket, grinning at me. When he grins I find myself thinking how fine it would be to kick him square in the face. He wore a white shirt, unbuttoned, the tails knotted across his flat brown belly. The gap in the shirt exposed the curly mat of hair on his hard brown chest. Christy calls him "that Errol Flynn, junior grade." He's got a brush-cut, amber eyes set tilty, a neat mustache, a white-toothed, knowing, wicked grin.

"It doesn't look like you're fresh out of money, Rigsby."

"It was a lovely house party. Charming people. A beautiful home near Naples. But they drink more than they should, doll. And when they drink they have this fantastic belief in their own ability to play gin and poker and whatall. Even Scrabble, hardly a game for wealthy illiterates."

"Why don't you just carry a gun?"

"I'd much rather be a house guest, Alice dear. I met them at Varadero last year and they said *do* come over and see us in Naples because now we're living there all year round. And this seemed like the time to go. People are so much more relaxed in the summer, don't you think?"

"You've paid your money and made your brag. I don't need conversation, Rex." He left, still grinning. You can't insult him. You can't dent his ego with a sledge. And, as some indignant husbands have learned, he's rough. He's quick and hard and he doesn't scare.

I don't know how old he is. You would think he's about thirty unless you took a close look at the skin under his eyes and on his throat and the backs of his hands. He makes a living as a tomcat. That's the most accurate way to put it. His ketch sleeps six. He knows the Bahamas the way most men know their own back yard. From the Abaco Cays to Turks Island. I've heard men who know the water say he's a fine sailor, but a little too bold. They say that whenever you find a man who loves to wear a turtleneck sweater and a sheath knife in port, it's certain he'll take a few more chances than he should.

He has a small income, I don't know where from. The *Angel* is always available for cruise charter, specialty, the Bahamas. He generally picks up a deck hand at Bimini after taking it across the Stream by himself. He advertises a little in the yachting magazines, but mostly he bird dogs the charters himself. And he has some friends alerted to hand out his cards to the right sort of customers, with a kickback if it goes through.

Rigsby picks and chooses. He won't take honeymooners, or an all-male charter, or a middle-aged couple. Christy said one time that she'd figured out the ideal charter for Rigsby. Five rich, handsome, restless women, all on trial separation from their husbands, all generous, vulnerable and semi-alcoholic, and with no tendency toward jealousy.

Sometimes the *Angel* will be gone so long we'll begin to hope he'll never come back. But he always does. It's an inexpensive mooring. Sometimes he'll lay over at Nassau and bird dog customers from there. He has the trick of getting himself invited on parties and house parties. It isn't much of a knack. All you have to have is gall. Somebody says, "You must come and see us sometime." Next thing they know, he's either pulling up to their dock, or turning into their driveway. It means free food, free liquor, gambling winnings and, generally, free women.

He's a small-souled man, but picturesque. When he takes the *Angel* out, all sparkling in the sun, with him brown and adventurous at the tiller, you can practically hear the music on the sound track and see the cameras panning on him.

His success with women who should know better is enough to make you sick. His score around here is only fair, however. Jannifer Jean, of course, which is about as much of a triumph as shooting a hen in a chicken yard. And Beezie Hooper, Stan Hooper's wife. Stan Hooper owns the *Fleetermouse* and keeps it in charterboat row, and he's licensed to run it as a charter fisherman, but that's only a tax dodge. It's too much boat to run it at a profit that way. And he lines up just enough charters a year to satisfy his accountants. He's loaded, and they have a big waterfront house north of town, and they live fast and hard, and party a lot. Beezie is scrawny and beautiful and mostly drunk. Stan found out about it and tried to make an issue of it, and got the hell beat out of him by Rex. They're the same size, but Rex's intake is two drinks a day instead of a fifth.

And he caught Amy Penworthy in a reckless mood. It

had rained for three days and poor Amy was so blue she didn't care what she did. So that hardly counts. And I'm not counting the women on the tourist boats. When three or four of them pull in, traveling together, and tie up close, and set up a party, Rex has a way of easing himself into the group, knowing that sooner or later, if he's careful and patient, he can talk some gal into walking around onto D Dock and taking a look at the way he's got the *Angel* fitted out below. Few men have ever had a better chance to combine their business and their hobby.

But he has been smart enough to stay away from Ginny Linder. And he has scored zero with Anne Browder, Christy and Helen Hass. He came close to getting to Helen. But she's such a serious, intense, humorless little thing, that it was taking him a long time to manage it—so long that the others caught on. Orbie and Lew went and had a little talk with Rex. They never let on what they said to him, but from then on Rex has stayed forty feet away from Helen. She looked wistful for a few days until she got over him.

Anne let on right away that she wouldn't dip him up a bucket of water if he was on fire. Christy played up to him. When she came up to my place with Gus and Orbie and Joe and told us about it, we all got laughing so hard we were crying.

It was late night and it happened on the dock. She let him kiss her. She dropped her cigarettes and when he reached for them, she accidentally stepped on his hand. And apologized something fierce. They walked out to the end of the dock. He kissed her again, and then her foot slipped, sort of pitching her forward so the top of her head hit him in the nose. He had to go change his shirt and she got an ice cube and held it against the back of his neck. He kept trying to get her aboard the *Angel*. They went out and sat on the fish box at the end of D Dock. She said he sort of soft-talked her until all her reserve was gone and then she turned and kind of plunged against him. He gave one yelp and went over backward into the water, about a seven-foot drop because the tide was way down.

She said that at that point she thought she could get one more chance at him, and having been raised with four older brothers, she had tricks he'd never heard of. It was just a case of keeping her voice under control while she apologized. But he floundered around in the water and said bitterly, "I'm wearing my new slacks and sandals, damn it all!" And that set her off. He got the message. He despises her. Nothing is so unforgivable to a tomcat man as to be laughed at by a girl he thinks has been taking him seriously.

The next day he left and was gone for almost a month. It must have been a good month. When he came back he bought the little Triumph.

No, I won't miss Rex, not a damn bit. But some I'll miss so bad it will hurt like an abscess. Gus, Orbie, Joe, Cindy, Jack, Jimmy, Lew, Amy. And I'll be alone again. That will be the worst of it. Except for the farm, and that was so long ago, this is the only place where I've put roots down, this rackety old sun-bleached marina.

I yawned. I felt sad and dead and old. I wished old Gus would chunk a pebble against my window so I could go down and let him in, so he could tiptoe up the stairs like a sneaky rhinoceros. It wasn't that I felt heated up, but just wanting somebody close to hold on to, and not feel so lonely. Just to hold that sweet, sturdy old clown, the third man in my life, and the last.

But that Annabelle daughter is in town with her husband and kids, walking around looking like she bit on something sour, taking Gus out to dinner every night and trying to get him to come live with them, and buying him old-man clothes. So he goes around looking solemn and grandpa-like, and he won't come near me until they've gone.

They want to take him back North and get him ready for death, but he isn't ready yet. There's youngness in him. A brawling, bawdy, roistering youngness. Like Christy says, Gus is like a Princeton freshman on vacation.

Where will Gus go when I sell? Damn all progress. Damn George and the Decklins and the syndicate and all the booster businessmen who want this eyesore marina torn down so there can be big concrete docks and uniformed men hustling ice and supplies in little motorized carts, and a big fancy restaurant and cocktail lounge. Already it's one city from Miami to West Palm, and they want every

59

part of it to look like every other part. You can hardly find Elihu Beach right now, even when you're looking for it.

I went to my window to take the last look of the evening at my shaky little empire. Midnight. Sid Stark's big Chris is lighted up again, all fifty-four of it. So they've come back to the boat after partying in town.

Further out along D Dock I could see a bright light moving around and realized it was Rex Rigsby checking the *Angel,* inspecting his lines. One thing he does is keep that ketch in as good shape as he keeps himself. Tools of his trade. He can't wait for daylight to check and see if Billy Looby did a good job of . . .

SIX

Rex Rigsby

. . . SANDING DOWN AND REVARNISHING the combing on this forward hatch. I told the old son of a bitch if it wasn't done right, I wouldn't pay for it. That's why I checked those bills so closely, to be certain he hadn't tried to put it through before I got a chance to look at it. It looks good. It looks as if he shaded it with a tarp like I told him.

I straightened up and clicked off the hand lantern and looked up at the mast tip making a six-inch arc against the stars. I could feel the tiny contented movement of her under my feet. My *Angel*. The only loyal one. The only true one. With the stick bowed and the rail under, the sheet hard as a drum and the wind hollering wild music through the stays, you have your own song, your own graceful dancing. And you're at your best when we're alone, the two of us. When there are others aboard, you sulk a little, respond a little less quickly, concealing yourself from me. I sense your disapproval, girl. Your delicate jealousy.

I went below, unpacked quickly and stowed everything where it belonged. Tapped the glass and watched it hitch up a half a tenth. Opened everything—she smelled a little bit musty below. Checked the battery level. It had held well with the new heavy-duty jobs. Tomorrow run the auxiliary and the generator, turn on the set and get the time signal and set the chronometer. Top off the water tanks and then check you over from bowsprit to transom, put a new shine on your fittings and sweeten the bilge.

61

But don't expect an early rising, *Angel* girl. Things have been strenuous. And profitable.

I stripped down, yawning, and sat on the edge of my bunk and counted the money. Just shy of eight hundred, after paying the bill. Good pay for long hours. I estimate three hours sleep a night for six nights. But with a nap every day, thank God. Even though that Karen wench cut the nap short a couple of times with that corny line about awakening the sleeping prince with a kiss. A kiss flavored with gin and stealth. She made her contribution, then wanted to cut for double of nothing. But I had the ace crimped, and she came up with cash. Sometimes they'll stop payments on checks.

Karen wasn't trouble. But that Maryanne was, after her Ralphie saw the way the ball was bouncing. I had to step lightly. Always remember that a house guest is unlikely to have a gun, but your host is very likely to have one around.

He probably figured out, correctly, it had started in Varadero. But he cased it wrong when he assumed I was coming around for more. Poor Maryanne just isn't that good, bless her. She's getting a bit long in the tooth. Ralphie could have guessed it was his D and B rating that brought me on the run, not Maryanne's whiney little love letters.

Ralphie finally decided to react harmlessly by drinking big and consoling himself with that anemic-looking Gretchen whose hubby in turn sought the usual revenge by successfully pursuing little Ruth, whose young husband went home mad.

All the familiar charades, poolside, beach and bedroom. The clumsy game of the idle rich. Musical beds. Sometimes I feel like a midget who, successfully impersonating a child, goes to all the birthday parties and wins all the prizes. Sometimes it seems too easy. Peek over the blindfold and pin the tail squarely on the donkey. There should be a pun in that somewhere.

Karen was very liberal about Maryanne. Said it was good for her, but it was not true tolerance, only the itch of the voyeur, readily satisfied.

And a charter came out of it too. Definitely a splendid charter. Louisa and her husband and her divorcee sister, for three weeks in September, with emphasis on Andros, Eleuthera and Spanish Wells. It was no trick to tell that Louisa had been properly alerted by her dear friend Karen. And perhaps has alerted her sister. The husband, whose name I cannot remember, is a dull man and an ardent fisherman. He won't be happy trying to fish off a ketch, and so that is the wedge. All three of them have that rich warm smell of money. Sisters can be amusing. And I have the check for a third of the charter. Earnest money, he called it. I gave them the class A rate. And the sisters will make another little gift of money—one way or another. Plus kickbacks from the places I take them. September should be a joyous month.

I turned off the light and stretched like a tiger in the wide comfortable bunk. My *Angel* sighed a little at her moorings as something went by on the Waterway and rocked her slightly. A few idle weeks coming up, before the charter. And two little games to play.

One game named Francesca Portoni, which could be dangerous, considering the hoodlum look of Sid Stark and his friends. But possible, if the look she gave me wasn't faked. And a second game named Judy Engly, chubby little Judy, she of the sensuous mouth and eyes of downcast sulky arrogance, she of the frantic ululations in the night, whooping and yelping—sounds of such great promise it prickles the backs of my hands and clinches the skin at the nape of my neck. Very possible, once she has been lured to a private place. It would not take words then—just hands and mouth and boldness. A game more desirable and less dangerous than the Portoni woman. The big mild fisherman husband was styled for the wearing of horns.

No more of the others here. No more of tiresome Beezie Hooper, leathery from sun and diet, all painful teeth and nails and knobs of bone, as violent in what should be a gentler art as a small boy in a picnic sack race. Certainly no further interest in rainy-day Amy, freckled as a trout, complaining of somebody named Milton, and complaining of the weather and her job at the bank, making it all as conversational and unremarkable as though we were rowing around in a dinghy, chatting. Positively no second event with the soiled Moonbeam who smelled of sweat and cotton candy, then blandly demanded ten dollars and used language that would shame a teamster when she didn't get it.

And, Rex, my boy, no attempts to rectify the times you struck out around here. Not with Hass, unless you want to be chopped into chunks and used for chum in barracuda water. Or with Browder, who is solid ice from her eyes to her deceptively dimpled knees. Nor with the Yale woman, the clown bitch, the comedian. I would like to watch her drown. I would like to use my fists and my heels on her, and turn that mocking face into something a buzzard wouldn't touch.

Just Francesca and Judy, both worthy of the stalk. Plus a prowl on the public beach from time to time, and a tour of the lounges, and the women on the transient cruisers. Fair game in my private jungle.

I should have felt a sense of anticipation for all the warm shy flesh of the girls in summer, honeyed by the sun, full of their fragrances, their transparent guiles and ploys. A youthful welcome change from the mannered decadences of the house-party wives with their veined hands, greedy eyes and fat pocketbooks, their frantic awareness of the passing of time, their emasculated husbands, their absentee children. At thirty feet they have the slimness and the bright hair and the vivacity of twenty-five. But the vivacity is the result of gin and tension, the bright hair is a dyed lifelessness, and the slimness is the result of constant hunger and dogged exercise. In the sleep of morning their heads lie heavily on the pillows, their faces are fifty and their bodies are stale and completely spent.

But I could not, this time, pleasure myself with anticipation of the young girls of the boats and beaches and lounges. I felt old and sour and bored.

And so, to hearten myself, I remembered how far I had come, how little there had been in the beginning. Not even the name. Drab section of a stinking Pennsylvania coal town. Hunky-Town they called it, and the name I had then fit the word. Six of us—God knows where the others are, and God also knows I don't care—and the father killed in a union brawl, and the mother, sour and leaden and sprawling with drink, honoring us with a new "uncle" every few months until she became so ill they took us all and put us in the Home, and herded us to her funeral a month later. I hated her. I still hate her, even dead. She was filth.

I went over the wall when I was sixteen, and I was on the bum for a year, a tough foul-mouthed clumsy quarrelsome kid before the Baron picked me up in San Francisco, cold, shabby and damn near starving. Maybe his title was good. Maybe he invented it. But he had the money to go with it.

We went to the south of France. He had a villa. Bought me clothes. Hired tutors. Taught me how to walk and talk, eat and drink. Treated me like a son, except in one department, and that not often. He was a tall frail old man who wept easily. I learned how easy it was to make him cry, to make him buy me presents. He bought me my first boat, and when I learned to handle her, it was as if I had been set free.

I was with him two years. When I found him dead on the bathroom floor—it was his heart—I cleaned all the francs and dollars and pounds sterling out of the safe. He never knew I had learned the combination. I buried the money in a zinc box in the garden and left the equivalent of a thousand in the safe so it wouldn't look too funny. Then I called his doctor.

His relatives threw me out of the place. They let me keep my clothes, but they took the boat. I moved into a little hotel. A week later I went back and got the money. I was nineteen but I looked older.

I went to Paris. There I met a raddled old movie actress named Maria who was as rich as the Baron and believed herself to be still glamorous. She took me back to La Jolla with her, brought some of my old-fashioned manners up to date, bought me a car, boat and clothes and gave me an abundant allowance. It was a better boat. It could really fly.

But she haunted me. She was after me every minute. She disgusted me. I kept telling her I was going to leave her. She would beg and cry and tell me how much she'd done for me. Finally she showed me her new will. She said her lawyer hadn't approved. She had me down for a nice chunk. I kept thinking about that money. One night she got thoroughly boiled. She would do that every once in a while, usually after we watched one of her old movies in the little projection room in the basement. It was February. The newspapers on the coast were complaining about the worst cold spell in years. Crop damage and all that. She was mumbling so badly I couldn't understand what she was saying. I went to her bedroom and found her sleeping pills and stole two of them. They were capsules. When she asked me to fix her a fresh drink, I dumped the contents of the capsules in it, stirred it up and took a sip. It was a little bitter, but not too bad. She drank it down.

Fifteen minutes later I tried, and I couldn't wake her up. I carried her to her bedroom, took her clothes off, and put her out on the little Spanish-looking balcony off her bedroom. Nobody could see her there. I shut the French doors to keep from cooling the house off, after I'd filled the big teakettle with cold water and wet her down good. Every hour I would go back and check on her and wet her down again. She didn't look very good. And I was nervous about the whole thing, thinking of all the things that might go wrong.

When the sky turned gray she had started breathing in an odd way. I carried her back in, dried her off, slipped her into one of her fancy nightgowns, tucked her into bed, and looked around, checking things. She had the script for every movie she'd ever made in a cabinet near the bed. She liked to read them after she was in bed. So I got one and fixed it so it looked as if she had been reading it. I turned off her light and went to my room and went to sleep right away. I was tired.

At about eleven the maid, who came every morning at nine, hammered on my door. I went with her to take a look at Maria. Maria was flushed, her hair damp with sweat, her forehead like a furnace. She looked at us with stary eyes and gobbled things that made no sense. I called the doctor. He gave her some shots and moved her to the hospital.

She lasted until about four the following morning. I was questioned. I told them she'd gotten a little stinko and had decided to take a midnight swim. The pool was full. They asked about a swim suit and I said that wasn't

66

the way she went swimming. They asked me why I didn't stop her. I said I was just a house guest. They didn't approve of me. The lawyer didn't think much of me either, but there wasn't anything he could do about it. Nobody was close enough to her to want to contest the will. So I got the money.

I knew that I'd probably spend it if I kept it around, like the Baron's money. I was smart enough to put it in a trust fund, and that's how I've been getting this income all these years. It won't buy what it used to buy, but it is very comforting.

I went to New York and found work as a male model. Ran around with a weird group. Tumbled a hundred girls. Resolved never to get myself tied up with anybody again. And got homesick for sailing. And found an absolutely safe way to stay out of the service.

I like to look at them when they cry. I like to hear them beg and plead and threaten to kill themselves. And I love to get them skunk drunk, so that they don't have any idea of what's happening, and you can despise them. Women are greedy, stupid animals, every one. During the war years, New York was too lush a hunting ground to leave. Too many of them wanted to be comforted. I perfected the techniques to such an extent that I kept four pals busy with my discards, improving their batting average by telling them what approach to use.

By 1946 I'd had enough. I came down here and bought that cranky sloop and learned the waters in her. And traded for that dog of a schooner which nearly drowned me. Then cleaned out that woman up in Fort Pierce and went over and had my *Angel* built on Abaco, just the way I wanted her.

So it has been a long time, Rex boy, and you've come a hell of a long way from Hunky-Town, so be of good cheer. Some rest is all you need. You're not ready for hormones yet.

Suddenly I remembered that in my eagerness to see how good a job Looby had done, I'd neglected to check my lines forward. I grunted with exasperation, pulled on my shorts and went topside with the light and checked. Everything looked fine. I took a look at the newcomer moored beside me, a Higgins by the look of the lines. I flicked the light along it, then went back below.

I was wondering how anybody could get much pleasure out of the water by churning along in a stinkpot cruiser. I even hate to use the auxiliary. I'll sail her in and out whenever I can. I don't know how a man can . . .

SEVEN

Leo Rice

. . . RUN A THING THAT SIZE with sails and stay in the
channel. It gives the man who can do it a disturbing
flavor of competence. Disturbing to me.

I sat up in the bunk and watched him when he first
started moving around on his boat with that light. I
didn't know he was back. Nobody knew when he was
coming back, and I couldn't make a point of asking directly.
At a house party, they said, over on the other coast. In
Naples. Rigsby is quite a man for house parties, they
told me.

I should have known from the picture the agency got
for me that he would look the way he does. The light reflected on him off the whiteness of the deck, and I saw
the hard blunt bones in his face, the taut bulge of his
shoulders, the muscular thickness of a forearm. I told
myself the picture had been taken a long time ago, and
that now he would be softer, older, more vulnerable—
not so hard and fit.

Were I objective enough, I would know perhaps how
childish I am being. Shoveling those tons and tons of sand
to bring the muscles back and slim away the executive
belly. Buying a boat and learning how to handle it. Playing his game instead of my own, and knowing I will
never be able to play it half as well as he. What in God's
name am I trying to prove? That I am a man?

Now he has gone back below for the second time, and
the light has gone out, and I can lay back. He is in a bunk
not unlike this one. He is perhaps thirty feet from me.
We lay in darkness with our separate thoughts. The dif-

ference is that he is totally unaware of me. And I am so completely aware of him that it seems impossible that he cannot sense it.

To him I am just another husband. A trivial obstacle. He's a careless animal, befouler, betrayer. Something to be killed. Retribution for something he did last year, in October and a part of November, and probably has not thought of it again.

Last year. Her last year. I don't know when it started to happen to Lucille. I thought everything was all right between us, just as it had always been. We'd been in the new house for five years. I was complacent, thinking our love was safe. It didn't have the magic and wonder of the first years. But does that ever last with anyone? And I had been working too hard for too long, I guess.

Over a year battling the details of the merger, fighting the tax case, and plugging for restyling of the entire line. I'd come home spent and irritable.

But I loved her. I didn't show it enough. I loved her. She was more beautiful at thirty-eight than when I married her, and almost as slim. Night-black hair and those sooty eyes and that slow mocking smile when she knew I wanted her. She'd made the effort to stay lovely for me. But I'd let myself go. That's one of the things you think about afterward. Thirty pounds overweight, with flabby gut, jumpy nerves, puffing on the stairs, slopping around unshaven in old clothes on holidays.

I was never unfaithful to her. Damn it, I never had the time, much less the inclination. When you move from store-room clerk to executive vice-president in eighteen years, in a company with two thousand employees, you haven't got time for games. Or enough time for your wife or kids. You bring work home and you sit with it until you can't keep your eyes open.

But it was all for her and the kids, wasn't it? Or was it? Was most of it because I wanted the joy of winning. It's the biggest poker game in the world.

I took her love for granted. I was proud of her and my home and the boys. But of course the entertaining we did had to be slanted businesswise. As well as most of the invitations we accepted. That's the way of the world. Accept it.

I thought she had accepted it.

Until that night almost a year ago. A sweltering night in Syracuse, but cooler out at our place overlooking the Tully Valley. The boys were at camp. Some people from Washington had been on my neck all day and I was emotionally exhausted from the strain of keeping my guard up. I showered and had two drinks to relax me, but not enough to spoil my concentration after dinner when I intended to go over the tabulations prepared by our comptroller. But I never got around to the tabulations that night.

After dinner she said she wanted to talk to me. She seemed very solemn, as though something had gone wrong. I wondered if she'd heard from her sister again. She wanted to talk out on the terrace. I felt impatient. I couldn't afford too long an interruption.

"I think this is important, Leo."

"What is it, dear?"

It was one of the long dusks of summer, just dark enough to make the sudden flare of her lighter quite vivid.

"I've been thinking about this a long time, Leo. I'd like to send the boys to boarding school in the fall."

I'd been prepared for something trivial, but this was not trivial at all. "Why!" I asked explosively. "They're doing so well. You keep telling me the school is pretty good."

"I know that this may sound peculiar and maybe selfish to you, Leo, but it isn't the boys, it's me."

"You?"

She sucked on the cigarette with such intensity it hollowed her cheeks. "Somewhere along the line I've lost part of myself. I don't know how. We've lost it, maybe. I know that in a couple of years the boys will be going away anyway. And maybe then it will be too late."

"Too late for what, for God's sake?"

"I knew you wouldn't understand. I feel—unused, darling. I'm sort of decaying in the middle like a tree or something. I look ahead at the years that are coming and I just feel bored. I shouldn't feel bored. It isn't right. So I want to go away for a while, and find out who I am and who I can become."

"You know I can't possibly—"

71

"I know that so well, Leo. So well. I didn't mean with you."

"Alone?"

"Not exactly. With Martha. By late September that will will be all be settled and she can get away."

Martha and Charlie Dade had been close friends. During the previous April Charlie had a coronary, neither mild nor severe. After three weeks in the hospital he had another one despite the anti-coagulants they were giving him, and it had killed him in minutes. Martha is a rangy, noisy, raw-boned blonde.

"You've talked this over with her?"

"Yes."

"Where would you want to go?"

"Nassau."

"For how long?"

"We don't have any idea. A couple of months, I think. You can't tell how long therapy will take."

I tried to talk her out of it. I made alternate suggestions. I couldn't move her an inch. I'd never seen her so stubborn. I finally said, trying to hurt her, "If this is a trial separation, the least we can do is be honest and call it what it is."

"You can call it anything you want, Leo. You can be just as inaccurate as you please. I tried to explain it to you. If you don't want to try to understand, I'm sorry. But I am going away for a while. If you don't want to pay the expenses, I can use the bonds Daddy left. I've never touched them, you know."

She won, of course. The boys were confused and upset. We got them into a good school. It seemed easier to close the house and live at the club down in town. I put her car in storage. I saw them off at the airport. I kissed her. Her lips were cool and firm, her eyes quick and nervous. I'd fixed her up with a thick stack of traveler's checks and a letter of credit at a correspondent bank in Nassau.

Thus began a period of unreality for me. I think my decisions were as sound as usual, my concentration as good. But I felt oddly remote. Sometimes it was hard to believe she was not home where she damn well belonged. I fought against nasty little images in my mind, created by jealousy. She was damned attractive. She wrote me dutifully once a week, stilted, almost formal letters. Like letters she might write to an uncle she did not know very well. And I wondered how well I knew her. I could have arranged to get away for a few days to fly down and see her and ask her to come home. But I was stymied by my own pride.

On October 16th I received the following airmail letter from her.

"By the time you get this, Leo, Martha and I will be off on an adventure. We have chartered a precious little sailboat called a ketch. It is named *Angel* and it's owned and captained by an American named Rigsby. He's going to sail us around to the other islands and teach us what ropes to pull on and so forth. We're very excited about it, as you can imagine. Martha is all packed and I'm not, so I must cut this short. Love, Lucille. PS. We were terribly lucky to find him free. He told us somebody else canceled out. I asked around, and they say he is a very good sailor and knows the Bahamas well."

The last I ever heard from her was a post card from Hatchet Bay, telling me that she loved sailing, and that the colors of the water were unimaginably beautiful.

On the fourteenth day of November I accepted a collect call at my office from a police official in Nassau who, after he had made certain of my identity, informed me that my wife was dead. He said she had apparently taken her own life, but he would not give me any further details. I remember very little about making flight arrangements or about the trip down. I went to the office of the man who had phoned me. The night before last she had locked herself in her room and taken an overdose of sleeping capsules. She had been in the hotel, alone, only two days. It had been obvious to the management that she had been drinking heavily. I stared at him. "She never drank heavily."

He shrugged. He was very polite, very helpful, very remote. He gave me the impression that he had seen so many American women do so many astonishing and unspeakable things that he had lost the capacity for surprise. There was no empathy left in him.

He checked all the likely hotels to see if a Martha Dade was registered. She was apparently not in Nassau.

He got Lucille's suitcases out of storage. The police had

packed her belongings. There had been no note. Her money was in an envelope, carefully sealed. A little over twenty dollars. No traveler's checks. A hotel bill had not been paid. He said if I would give him the money, he would take care of it for me. He gave me a receipt. There were intricate forms to be filled out and signed. He took me to where she was. I looked down at dulled black hair and the slack face of a dead stranger. She was heavily tanned, but it had a greenish, yellowish cast. Her face was far too thin, with pouches under her closed, sunken eyes.

She was flown back in a cargo plane for the horrid ceremony of funeral and burial. The boys could not be consoled. Their safe warm life had been fragmented.

After they were back in school I traced Martha to Bimini. I flew down. She was a guest aboard a huge yacht out of Miami. She was half-drunk and slightly sullen and strangely indifferent. Yes, she had heard of Lucille's death. Too bad, she said, but she didn't seem particularly moved.

"Why did you split up?" I demanded.

She shrugged so violently some of her drink spilled into the concrete quay. She was squinting in the hot sunshine. Her shoulders were peeling. "I got myself dropped off at Rock Sound. On the twenty-second of October. End of cruise for little Martha."

"Why? Was there a quarrel?"

"Do you have to have it all spelled out for you, Leo? Should I draw pictures? It got too cozy aboard the *Angel*. Three's a crowd. Yes, there was a quarrel. A dirty one. She was having all the fun and games, and I was the maiden aunt and I didn't like it."

"But Lucille wouldn't—"

She looked at me flatly, with animosity. "She did, old buddy. Eagerly and frequently. With bells on, after Rex got her conscience quieted down. The first time was not exactly rape, but she cried and carried on about it. After that it all got too damn cozy. The wide blue sea is a romantic place, Leo. And don't blame her too much. You have to understand that, like two goofs, we'd put ourselves in the hands of a greedy, adept, merciless son of a bitch."

I flew from there to Nassau looking for Rigsby. The *Angel* was gone. I found out it had been docked at Yacht

Haven. I hung around until, by luck, I found a man who had seen the next to the last chapter of the story, and remembered it well, probably because it had bothered him.

Rigsby had been aboard the *Angel* at dusk, with a young couple. A dark-haired woman had come out onto the dock, visibly wobbly with drink. She had stood beside the *Angel*, begging and pleading with Rigsby. My informant hadn't been able to hear her very well. It had been something about love and something about money. Rigsby answered her curtly. The man had heard him telling her to go away, she was boring him. She continued the scene. People on other boats were watching. Finally Rigsby had bounded up onto the dock and slapped her so hard he knocked her down. She got up slowly, without a sound, and walked away. That was the night she had killed herself.

It is difficult for me to explain what this information did to me. Lucille had always been a woman of style and poise and dignity. He had dirtied all that. In that, and in other ways, he had made it impossible for her to live with herself, much less come back to me.

I went back home with that sour knowledge heavy on my heart. I told myself it was over. I told myself it was no more her fault than if she had been run over by a truck. It was my inattention that had made her nervous and vulnerable. Aboard the *Angel* they had been a pair of rabbits in the cave of the panther.

I tried to throw myself into my work with such intensity I could blank out that part of my mind which concerned itself with her. Hard work had become tasteless. Finally, telling myself that if I knew more about Rigsby, I would get over it more quickly, I put a top firm of investigators on him and paid them a great deal of money to do a thorough job. They couldn't trace him back to his origins. It was an ordinary-sounding account.

He had no police record. It was only by reading between the lines that you could detect the stink of him. Three times he had been named corespondent in divorce suits. He was a brawler, and twice had put men in the hospital, but no charges had been filed. He used Elihu Beach as his home port and kept the *Angel* at the Stebbins' Marina.

The summary was very cautiously worded. They said

that even though there was no police record, it was considered possible that Rigsby was unscrupulous in money matters, particularly where women were involved. It was believed that it was his habit to borrow sums of money from women with whom he became emotionally involved, and make no effort to return such sums when the affairs were terminated. In addition to Lucille, there had been three other suicides among his intimates, two female and one male.

I read the report so many times that I inadvertently committed long passages to memory.

And I began to make mistakes in my work. Not crucial ones, but it was a warning that sooner or later I would make one so large it might negate the progress of years.

I knew then that I had to go after Rigsby. It had become obsessive. It took over three months to so organize my work, splitting up duties and responsibilities, that I could ask a leave of absence from the Board, reasonably certain that my executive assistant could carry on throughout the summer. I talked to Sam Brayman who handles my personal legal matters. I had decided he would be the only one who would know how to contact me. Sam was horrified.

"Good God, Leo, you gone out of your mind? Don't talk to me. Talk to a psychiatrist. You pick a fake name like Rice, and make like the secret service sneaking up on that guy. What the hell do you expect to do?"

"I don't know, Sam. I don't want him to know who I am. I don't want him to make the connection. I want to meet that animal face to face."

"And then what?"

"There must be some way to put him out of the woman business."

"You're not thinking straight, Leo." He stared at me. "Suppose you can't fix his wagon for him. You going to kill him? I'm your lawyer. It's a fair question."

"I don't know. I've thought of that. I might."

"Thats just fine. That will be great for the boys. Give them a hell of a fine start in life, reading how their daddy was hung."

"They'll have the trust fund you're setting up, Sam. And I'm not much good to them the way I am. I'm not much good to anybody. I'm not very damn interested in living. I didn't know how much she meant. And she deserved better than what he gave her. Or I gave her. I have to see him, Sam. I want to see if I can get him to talk about her. I want to hear *how* he talks about her. I want to see what he is, what motivates him. I don't want to have to kill him. I don't even know if I could, given a fair chance. I'm not rational about this. I admit it. Maybe if I could beat hell out of him, it might be enough."

He looked at the snap of Rigsby again. "This fellow looks pretty husky," he said dubiously.

"I'll be in shape by the time I meet him. I'll give myself time for that."

"As your attorney I—oh, the hell with it."

I made the arrangements about communication with him. Then I left.

Getting in shape was torture, self-inflicted. Not a case of swimming and jogging up and down the beach, though I did that too. I shoveled sand until sweat blinded me, my back was like a toothache, my shoulders popped and creaked. At the limit of endurance I would think of him knocking her down while people watched, and I would keep on shoveling. I lived on steak and salad. I'd fall into bed and clamber out of it again in the morning, with monstrous effort. In the evenings, after I was able to stay awake, I read the books there had never been time for. In a month I was ready. I bought the boat and chugged south, looking for Rigsby.

Now he was thirty feet away. I couldn't sleep. My mind kept racing and I couldn't slow it down. I got up. I was stiff and sore from the beating I had taken. Western had handled me with ridiculous ease. Rigsby would probably find me no more difficult. I sat on the rail and put a cigarette between puffed lips. Tomorrow I would see him by daylight, look into the eyes which had looked at her, look at the hands and lips of the last man to touch her while she lived.

She hadn't been bad or weak. Just restless and neglected. Particularly vulnerable. He had a fine eye for vulnerability. I wondered how many men had thought of killing him.

It gave me a feeling of hopelessness. I was just another

one. I'd think of it, as others had, and go my way in bitterness. He would go on, cruel and blithe, all the world his harem. An unmarked animal.

I snapped my cigarette out into the black water and heard the soft hiss as it struck. I went to bed hoping I could sleep . . .

EIGHT

Anne Browder

. . . AND SLEEP and never wake up, ever.

I sat cross-legged at dusk on a Wednesday night up on the foredeck of the *Alrightee* where no one could see me from the dock. I was celebrating a twelfth anniversary— twelve nights since I had indulged myself in fiasco with Joe Rykler.

The poor darling. No man has ever been so ill-used by a woman. I selected him in such a horribly cold-blooded way, adding up the advantages of him. He is amiable and amusing and sometimes sweet, and possibly slightly weak. He has been twice married. I have never heard him make one of those greasy little hints about a woman. He was interested in me. And I saw sensitivity in him, a capacity for understanding.

So I walked around him, kicking his tires, slamming his doors, peering under his hood—and took him for a demonstration ride.

Poor Joe. I was dead. I was a zombie. A few times I felt a dim flickering of a response, gone as soon as it was noticed, like striking damp matches in a rain. It all seemed endless, and it had a nightmare quality about it, as though I found myself engaged in some muscular and incomprehensible activity and, out of social timidity, did not dare ask, What on earth are we doing? My mind divorced itself primly from our barren, embarrassing efforts, and went skittering off into montages of trivia. Had I remembered to change Mrs. Milroyd's appointment on the books? Will the cleaners get my gray skirt back by Saturday so I can wear it to work Monday? I wish Amy would stop wearing my blue robe when she goes up to take a shower, but how can I tell her in a nice way?

And from these diversions I would return suddenly to the bunk aboard Joe's *Ampersand,* and be quite shocked to find myself in the midst of love, with a very small L. It reminded me of my first dancing class, when that horror of a Sherman boy used to come galloping over to me so he could push me about the floor like I were a wheelbarrow, and I would shut my eyes and pretend I was the only girl pitcher they let into the major leagues.

Not that Joe was a horror. He was determined and sensitive and knowing and adept. But he could have spent the same amount of time just as profitably trying to row D Dock out to sea with a popsickle stick, or is that illusion uncomfortably Freudian, my girl.

Were I younger, and had it been my first adventure in that ultimate art of being a woman, it would have terrified me. My frigidity would have appalled me. But, oh Brad, my darling, you know and I know that there is no danger of that. At times I almost frightened you, I know. And certainly shocked you. Then suddenly you were gone, and there was a spoiled, trivial little man, his mouth working, his forehead sweaty.

Poor little man, who had such a neat system for having his cake and eating it too that he was quite unprepared for ptomaine. It was as though all the time we were together I had been looking at your shadow on one wall of my heart, a shadow made large by the placement of the light. I thought the shadow was you, until with that movement of fright, you attracted my attention and I looked at you squarely and suddenly despised you, despised myself, and found our little apartment cloying and silly in its manufactured atmosphere of sensuousness.

However I have learned one thing of no value from Joe. Perhaps every woman at some time in her life has a little nibbling of curiosity about what it would be like, really, to be a whore, to give herself with automatic proficiency to any taker. That curiosity has been satisfied. I would be a dismal flop, Joe. They'd give me the worst room and the oldest bed and the most threadbare towels.

But why, Joe, oh why could you have let yourself think

you have fallen in love with me? How is it possible, after that night twelve nights ago? Love can't start that way. I chose you because I thought you would not become emotionally implicated. I could not bear to hurt anyone. Not after the way I've been hurt. I can't love you. Or anyone. To even attempt to would be like an old fighter getting back in the ring. They beat my brains out, dear. I can't take another punch.

So you follow me about with sad brown eyes now, and you say alarmingly poetic things to me. I never thought you would be vulnerable as a high-school boy.

Joe, you are in love with the idea of love, not me. That's why you married twice. Take a better look at me, darling. I'm a special kind of walking wounded. They sent me back from the aid station. They said, This girl's heart looks chewed, as though something ate half of it and bruised the rest of it black. Something emptied her eyes and disconnected certain primary sensory areas.

I messed us up, Joe, not out of mischief, but out of an instinct for self-preservation. I wished to manufacture a distraction, and was not at all distracted in the manner planned, as you surely noted.

And in twelve nights my remorse has not diminished. It is not the remorse one feels from having done something dirty wrong. Remorse, rather, for involving another. Had I known the experiment would have been so resoundingly unsuccessful—which is, of course, specious nonsense—I would have chosen Orbie, that tough, sane, cynical, tidy redhead. No nuances there. It would have been a briefer interlude, with Orbie not particularly concerned whether I chose to be bystander or participant. But he would not have become involved, and I would not now feel toward him that uncomfortable responsibility I feel toward you, Joe Rykler.

It is a special torment to be unloved in a lovely place. Now the last dusk colors are gone, the water gray as tears, the high neon feeble against what is left of the light. The heavy air is laced with fish and tide, rope and varnish, sun-hot wood and airborn salt, along with an elusiveness of flowers and tropic growth. All my senses work sharply, in either loneliness or love. Brad said I had a special talent for being alive. Out in open water

81

a boy in a snarly little boat is trying to dump a golden gawky girl off her water skis while she caws her derision.

Of what use is my talent?

I got up slowly. My legs were cramped from staying so long in one position. I walked along the side deck toward the stern. This evening they were grouped near the stern of the *Lullaby,* a big group because five of Orbie's current harem, the younger ones, are part of it. I heard the bassoon bray of Gus's laughter. He is himself again. His daughter and her family left this morning, sooner than expected, probably because of what happened yesterday.

Christy told me about it. She heard it from Billy Looby. He was the only witness to the entire incident, though others saw some of the dramatic parts of it. Poor Jannifer Jean. Poor Moonbeam.

A little motor cruiser came in yesterday morning from Fort Myers. One man aboard, proud of making it in two days. When he arranged dockage, he told Helen Hass it would only be overnight. He'd brought the boat over through the canal and the lake. His wife and another couple were flying over, and they were going to go down to the Keys and around and up the west coast, back to Fort Myers. He hung around in a sort of restless way. In the early afternoon he went up to the office. Moonbeam was watching afternoon television. He watched it with her and talked with her—a feat beyond my understanding. And, inevitably, apparently asked her if she'd like to come look at his boat.

They were still aboard when the wife arrived, alone. Christy said Billy told her he thought Helen sent her right on out there to C Dock just to make trouble. Christy also said there is no sign that Billy didn't enjoy the trouble when it came. He is a cackling, dirty, salacious old man, a voyeur, a tattletale and a sneak. But in some totally incomprehensible way, likeable.

Billy told Christy that not more than six seconds after the wife went aboard, Moonbeam came out of that little cruiser like a hooked tarpon. She had her tight pants in one hand and her shirt in the other. The wife was six feet behind her, making a noise like a factory whistle, and making slashing motions with something that glittered in the sunlight.

Billy said that Jannifer Jean, naked as a peeled egg and running for her life, was one of the most astonishing things he had ever been privileged to watch. The noise had alerted everybody within eyesight, and they all stood transfixed.

Moonbeam had more speed out of the gate than the wife, and when the gap had widened, the wife stopped. Moonbeam looked back and stopped too, and tried to get into the pants, hopping around on one leg. When the wife saw that, she came churning on again, and Moonbeam had to show her best speed.

They went through the same act again, but when Moonbeam loped off the third time, she veered out onto D Dock and leaped aboard Gus's *Queen Bee* and dived below. She was apparently looking for refuge, Christy said, on the basis of instinct rather than reason. But it must have seemed most remarkable to Gus, his daughter, his son-in-law and his two grandchildren when Jannifer Jean made her informal entrance.

After a few words which withered the flowers in Alice's flower boxes, the wife trudged back to the family cruiser. A minute later Moonbeam appeared again, clad in her own fashion, obviously wary. She sauntered up toward her trailer. And a minute after that, a subdued little group left Gus's boat and filed toward the parking lot. Billy said Gus was waving his arms and making explanatory noises, his face the color of new bricks.

How simple it would be to be a Moonbeam. Or Joe's Francie. How simple it would be to be almost anybody except me. Even little Judy Engly. But Christy said she saw Judy with Rex Rigsby over on the beach on Sunday in one of those open-air bars. Jack had a charter. Maybe Judy will not be finding it so easy to be Judy one of these days.

I walked up to the group. Lew asked me where I'd been hiding. Orbie introduced me to the two girls in the group I hadn't met. Leo Rice was in the group. And Gus and Amy and Alice and Dave Harran, who is welcome even though his employer, Dink Western, isn't. Dave got me a pillow off the stern deck of the *Mine,* and opened me a beer. He is a simple, gentle, decent, courtly man who served twelve years for murder.

It was only after I was seated that I noticed Rex Rigsby in the group. Usually we manage to chill him away from us. I decided that, because the presence of the five female employees of Bitty-Beddy, our normal coziness had already been fractured, and so it didn't seem worthwhile denting Rex's ego enough to make him leave. But it would make it more difficult to get rid of him the next time.

To Orbie's obvious annoyance, Rex had hunched himself close to the best looking girl of the five, and was speaking directly into her ear in a voice inaudible to the rest of us. She sat with downcast eyes, plucking at the hem of her shorts. God only knows what he was saying to her.

I did not want to ask where Joe was. There was no need to ask. He was beside me twenty seconds later, saying, "I leave for two minutes and the magic works. I rubbed the right lamp."

"Joe," I said.

He leaned so close to my ear I felt the warmth of his breath. "You're beautiful, Annie."

"Shush, Joe."

The second best looking of the Bitty-Beddy girls, a bosomy little towhead with a rather long upper lip, said, across the circle, with telling petulance, "And I was saving your place and guarding your can of beer, Joey."

"Hand it over, Cindy, please." He stretched and got it. "Thanks." She sniffed at him.

Lew started to tell one of his Navy lies. It gave us a little area of privacy. I slid the pillow back a little and said, "I interrupted something."

"Nothing that wasn't entirely her idea, honest."

"Make it your idea too, Joe."

"That's a funny thing to say."

"She looks clean and healthy and lonesome. She came down to have a mad gay time, and it hasn't worked out that way and she only has three days left, and she's getting nervous. Romance her, Joe. She can blame her indiscretion on the effects of the tropics," I whispered to him.

"My God, Anne. My God! Line four of the most gorgeous creatures two on a side in a bed for five, and I'd lay sick in the middle, dreaming of you."

"That's little-boy talk. I feel sixty to your fourteen.

And we didn't work at all, Joe. Remember?"

"I love you."

"Francie was one answer. Cindy can be another."

"It was different then. That was ten thousand years ago."

"You've got to get over this."

"I don't want to."

I turned and looked directly at him. "I might get you over it."

"What do you mean?"

"I might do something that doesn't fit your pretty little vision of me, Joe."

"Like?"

I raised my shoulders, let them fall. "Like Rigsby."

Even in that faintest of gray lights, I saw his face darken. "You couldn't do that! You couldn't!"

"Do you think I really, basically give a damn what I do?"

"Yes, Annie."

"You're wrong. And what would it mean, anyway. No more than with you. With him I'd feel afterward like taking a bath in Clorox, but if that's what's needed to put you off—"

"Are you trying to drive me out of my mind?"

"I'm trying to drive you back into your mind, Joe."

"You could love me. Give it time. Don't do anything that will bitch us up forever."

"I've been bitched up."

"But not by Rigsby."

I looked across the circle. Just then Billy turned the feeble dock lights on. Rigsby was gone, as was the pretty girl he had been talking to. Deftly done. I hadn't seen them leave and I doubted many others had. Cut neatly out of the herd with a clean loop over the horns and a masterful tug in the intended direction. A sour little something in my stomach turned over.

"All right," I whispered to Joe. "Not Rigsby."

"Not anyone."

"I didn't say that. I want to drive you away."

"I want to marry you."

"Go to your nearest department store. Buy a dummy out of a show window. Marry her, Joe. She'll be as alive as I am."

He clasped his fingers around my ankle, caressed the

85

back of my leg with his thumb. "Nothing?"

"Nothing at all."

He took his hand away. "It's a temporary thing. It's a psychological thing, Annie. Result of emotional trauma."

"It's a forever thing."

"If you don't care what you do, put it to the proof again, Annie. If it doesn't mean anything, what can you care?"

"I could drive our houseboat through the hole in that logic, my boy."

"Then what do I do?" he asked helplessly.

"There's Cindy over there, wondering if she'll have to tell lies to her girl friends when she gets back to Pennsylvania."

"Damn you, Anne. Damn you."

"I am damned. I have been. It's a good word."

"And you enjoy feeling *so* sorry for yourself."

"That's a foul thing to say!"

"Think it over," he said, and got up. He moved over by Leo and Cindy and started talking to them, as if I no longer existed. I started to feel a little hurt until suddenly I realized that was exactly what I wanted.

I looked over at Cindy. I could see her taking new heart. She got herself a beer and, with an epic casualness, turned it into a group of four. I watched them. She sat beside Joe, hugging her knees. Soon she was leaning her knees against him. When he made a joke she threw her head back and laughed hugely at the stars. Joe's back was toward me. I got up and . . .

NINE

Christy Yale

. . . QUIETLY WALKED AWAY. I wonder why she did that. She has been acting strange lately. Maybe I should say she has been acting stranger than usual. More curious. She and Joe. Like lovers who have quarreled. But that is impossible, knowing Anne.

When she first came, Joe vectored in on her like a one-man air force. He put on all his acts. He tried everything short of clubbing her over the head and dragging her away, but nothing worked. You could tell when he gave up, regretfully.

But this is not like that. Before, he had all the cheery optimism of a small boy chinning himself for a new girl in the neighborhood. Now he's jumpy and sour and moody. And she does not seem to be so carefully controlled. Ever since that night they went out together, surprising all of us, and probably Joe most of all.

Could it be possible that they . . .

Christy, my girl, you are all nose lately. Don't fuss with other people's problems. Content yourself—as somebody said—with the terrible geometry of your own.

And why should I think of Leo when I think of my own areas of concern? Possessive little wench.

But he's been so good to talk to and be with. And what in the foolish hell have we talked about these evenings we've been together? The right kinds of bait, and how birthdays were when you were little, and how far away the stars are, and why are cars so big, and how firm should we be with Russia, and what is a white lie, and why the sack went out, and why waterfront should cost so much.

I don't clown for him, or when he's around, and I don't get the same bang out of my little acts when he isn't around. I feel guilty, somehow. And—pathetic as it may seem—I am getting terribly girlish these days, trying to do something human about my hair, and pondering what to wear as though it was something crucial. I respond to him, because he's so damnably nice.

Not a word said yet about why he's here. But I know it has something to do with our Rex.

I don't think anybody else suspects Leo isn't exactly what he seems to be, a businessman taking a vacation for the sake of his health. But when he clued me that something was up, I was alert. That nose again. Such a pathetic little button of a nose, too.

First I had suspicions, and then I got the confirmation last Monday night, when I got my hand held and he didn't even know he was holding it. He nearly mushed it like stepping on a cookie, too.

Like this. I'd heard he'd buddied up to Rex. Apparently nobody had given him the message about that louse. And I was going to make it my business. Leo crewed half a day for Lew on Monday. I had to work late at the old C of C, so late that I ate in town, and it was dark when I got home to D Dock. Helen, for once, was home aboard the *Shifless,* but no company because she was studying her Spanish idioms. It was either get out or wind up holding the book and prompting her. I changed to shorts and a blouse and went out. Went ashore, if you're a nautical type. I wandered out toward the *Ruthless.* Casual little old me. Not really a pursuit, like the Tiger Lady looking for meat. Damn it, I like to be with the guy, and it seems reciprocal.

No lights on the *Ruthless.* The end of the dock has no light at all. Hasn't for months. Billy hasn't gotten around to putting in a new bulb.

Just as I turned sadly back, he said, "Hey, you!" He was sitting out on the fish box, scene of Rex's humiliation that time. With an enormous effort of will, I kept myself from jumping in the air and clicking my heels.

I went and sat beside him and said, "Am I pursuing you, sir?"

He laughed softly. "Haven't seen you batting your eyelashes."

"You know, Leo, when I first started reading everything I was big enough to pick up, that phrase, batting her eyelashes, worried me half to death. I used to wonder if genuine sirens carried a little stick they used. And I learned some mighty big words. Chaos was one I learned. Only in my mind I pronounced it chowse. So one day I showed off in history class. 'Europe is in a state of chowse,' I said. 'Chowse?' the teacher said. 'Complete chowse,' I said firmly. So she made me spell it. Then she practically had to be helped from the room. It was mighty humiliating, I can tell you true."

"I remember putting my mother into a state of semi-hysterics with the word bedraggled. I told her one morning at breakfast she looked a little bedraggled. Only I pronounced it bed-raggled."

"Oh my gosh! There was another one I—"

Just then Rex came up onto the dock off the *Angel* and stood and fired up his pipe. He smokes a pipe as though he were posing for a picture of the author on the back of a novel.

"Hi, Rex," Leo said.

"Oh, hello there, Leo," Rex said with that patronizing joviality of his that makes me want to spit. He strolled out toward us. When he got close enough to recognize me, he dug his heels in. He wants no part of me.

"Sit down, Rex, sit down," Leo said. "Christy, Rex has been telling me some of his adventures."

"I can imagine," I said.

Rex sat down, but on the other side of Leo, and with a certain reluctance.

"We were talking about Nassau the other day, yesterday I guess it was."

"Charming spot," Rex said, a bit of limey creeping into the A in charming. "Quaint, clean, romantic. I tie up there often. Yacht Haven when I have a charter. Hurricane Hole across the way when I'm paying the bills. Makes a difference. Inconvenient on the other side, though. Have

89

to dinghy over after the mail and so on."

"I suppose though," Leo said casually, "it could be a dangerous place for a woman alone." It was said very casually, but something in the timbre of his voice brought me to attention. It was like walking through a sleepy glade and hearing the celluloid whir of a rattler not far away.

"I don't see how," Rex said. "Marvelous police force."

"I guess I mean emotionally dangerous," Leo said. And, in a way that I knew was entirely unconscious, he took hold of my hand in the darkness and held it tightly. "Friends of ours in Syracuse. Acquaintances, I guess you'd call them. The Harrisons. Last year Lucille Harrison took a vacation in Nassau, and killed herself there."

"That's the damndest thing!" Rex said.

"How do you mean?"

"Small world department, Leo. Tell you about it." He took his time getting his pipe going again. "I knew the lady. Quite a handsome brunette, was she?"

"That's right." His grip was becoming uncomfortable.

"Heavy drinker, though. So many of them are. She and a friend of hers chartered the *Angel*."

"They did?"

"They certainly did. But it was cut short. The girls had a terrible quarrel. Liquor and so on. I had to put the blonde ashore on Eleuthera and take Mrs. Harrison on back to Nassau. Yes, I heard she did herself in. I'd forgotten that."

"Would you have any idea why?"

"Not the foggiest. She seemed like a sort of disorganized kind of person to me. Do you know, she came down to Yacht Haven half drunk and began whining to me about money I was supposed to owe her. Made a scene that nearly lost me a charter. She thought that because the charter ended before it was supposed to, she should have a refund or something. But I gave up another charter to take them, and I am definitely not in business for my health."

"About that quarrel, Rex. Could it have been over you?"

Rigsby chuckled. I could tell from the sudden movement of Leo's body that Rex had nudged him. And when Rex spoke, there was delicate slime on every word. "I wouldn't care to say right out, you understand. But you can guess how it is, old boy. They take their little marital vacations, and what they have in mind they make abundantly clear to an old sea wallah. It's a bit of a change for them after their businessmen husbands. One has to oblige, you know. One might even say it's part of the charter."

Leo's hand clamped on mine with such force that I couldn't even yell. "Too bad about that Mrs. Harrison. Quite pretty. But awfully emotional." He looked at the luminous dial of his mariner's watch, and stood up. "Have to be getting on. Fine sort of an evening, isn't it? Good night."

Leo said good night in a rusty voice. I couldn't say a word. Suddenly the pressure on my hand was gone. I found my hand still worked, to my surprise.

"Next time I want my hand held, I'll get somebody to run over it," I said.

He didn't answer. He sat like a clod. Suddenly he wrenched himself around, sprawled face down across the fish box, and began vomiting into the yacht basin. After two seconds of paralysis, I trotted to the *Ruthless* and went aboard, found the light and the towels. I soaked one in cold water and wrung it out, and took him that one and a dry one. He was almost through by the time I got back. He rested for a little while, then turned back and sat up. I gave him the damp towel. He muttered his thanks. He was shivering in the hot night. He sat with his face buried in the towel for a few minutes, knees on his elbows. I gave him the dry towel when he was ready.

"Now what was that all about?"

"A questionable hamburg," he said. "Done in by elderly meat, by God."

If he didn't want to tell, I wasn't going to press him. I had my confirmation. And a sore hand. He sagged with a weariness I knew was emotional. I sent him to bed. I went back and helped Helen check herself out on the idioms.

That was two nights ago. If I needed any further confirmation, which I don't, I got it tonight. Sitting beside Leo, on the side toward Rex, I was aware of the intensity of his interest in Rigsby. When ole Rex was sweet-mouthing the Bitty-Beddy girl, Leo leaned closer to me. I was not over-

91

come. He was trying desperately to overhear what Rex was saying to the girl. The interest was strong and abnormal and had a flavor of animal about it. It was a jungle interest that flattened his eyes and narrowed his mouth and bunched the corners of his jaw. After I decided Leo wasn't hearing a word of my prattle, I checked it out by saying, in the middle of one of my C of C stories, "Two of my brothers slew each other with their hula hoops yesterday."

"Uh-huh," he said.

Shortly thereafter Joe Rykler moved in on us, just moments after Rex eased off into the night with the queen of the Bitty-Beddy gals, when Orbie wasn't looking. It surprised me to see Joe leave Anne alone and sit with his back toward her. She went away too, but alone. And calmly.

The second best Bitty-Beddy gal moved in on us. Delicately. Like a home-made steam shovel. She had decided Joe was utterly nifty. Her approach was as subtle as Milton Berle. She merely leaned on him, breathing somewhat damply. Joe hitched away from her. She came along like she was attached. He tried again and couldn't detach her. Joe wore a pained and alarmed expression, like an awkward dinner guest who discovers he's been eating his neighbor's salad. He looked back over his shoulder at the place where Anne had been, perhaps with the idea of appealing for help.

"She's gone!" he said.

"Show me your cutey little boat, Joey," the Bitty-Beddy blonde said, sugary as all get-out. "What's the name mean anyhow? *Ampersand.*"

"The printers sign for 'and.' That thing that looks a little like a capital S."

"And. That's cutey. You *and* me, huh?" She nuzzled his shoulder like a kitten.

Joe bounded up so suddenly she nearly toppled over into the vacuum. "I—I got to go make a phone call." He walked away.

Miss Comptometer of the Year glared after him. She lit her cigarette with a violent slash of the match, glowered at me and said, "What the hell is with the men around here, Sis?"

"They're horribly shy," I told her.

"I could end up with lousy morale. I could end up think-

92

ing I'm a dog's dinner. My God, the passes I fight off in the office." She looked speculatively at Leo. I saw her begin to light up for him like a four-dollar furnace.

"Knock it off, dear," I said gently.

She sighed and got up and dusted the seat of her shorts. "They call this a vacation," she said. "Orbie, I'm going to walk back to the motel and wash my hair. Then maybe I'll go out and buy myself a drink and a sandwich. Big deal."

She walked down the dock toward shore, putting her heels down hard.

"Thanks," Leo murmured. "She was a little scarey."

I could sense the change in him. Before Rex left, I was just a nearby thing, like our inevitable tin washtub of beer, filled each night by public subscription according to each person's estimate of his own capacity. Or like one of the dock lights, or one of the folding chairs. With Rex gone, the tension had gone out of him, the animal waiting, the oddly feral curiosity.

"Welcome back," I said.

"What?"

I didn't have to try to explain, because at that moment forty feet of Custom Fisherman, handled with unmistakable smartness, came swinging between the markers, her running lights glowing, the big spotlight on the bow swinging across us and then focusing on the right slip over in charterboat row.

"Sim and Marty," Orbie said.

"Who?" Leo asked.

I stood up. "You haven't met them. They've been off on a long Bahama charter. Come on over and meet them. They're dolls."

Sim Gallowell and Marty Urban, co-owners and operators of the *Sea Gal* are the Crunch and Des of our little world. They have five kids between them, a duplex on the northwest edge of town, a pair of nice wives who take turns working while the other one takes care of the combined brood.

As we walked around with the others, Sim whipped the *Sea Gal* quickly and delicately into her slip, as only a pro can do it, gave the engines a few bursts and cut them. By then Marty had the lines just right. Somebody turned on their shore-side floods for them, bathing the gray and white boat in brilliance. Sim started rigging the rub rails while Marty hooked up their house to wash her down. They were naked to the waist, a sea-going brown against the pale boat, grinning and kidding with the spectators.

"How'd you really do?" Captain Jimmy asked. "I maybe got me a one-week charter for Bimini."

Sim straightened up from a crouch, fists on his hips, squinting in the lights. "I tell you, we left three happy guys off in Miami this afternoon. Out of the whole time we had three bad days, and that was weather. We hit it good everywhere we went, and it was best right off the Berrys, and second best down the Andros Shelf. We got one we're checking through for a record. Forty-one pound Permit on thirty pound test."

"Rough coming back across the Stream?" somebody asked.

"No place for anybody with a loose pivot tooth," Marty said. "On the way down we kept a-meeting ourselves on the way back up. One time there Sim got the color of a dollar bill."

"Where's your reception committee?" Lew hollered.

Sim grinned. "This time it's a surprise. They don't expect us in until tomorrow."

The little crowd dispersed slowly. I waited with Leo while they hosed her down, snapped the cockpit tarps in place and came ashore with their gear and turned off their floods. They weren't wasting any time. They wanted to pile into that junk jeep of theirs and head for home.

"Sim, I want you to meet Leo Rice, a new member of D Dock. Sim Gallowell and Marty Urban. He's been crewing for Lew off and on."

They shook hands. I saw Sim measure him and then give the grin that was the stamp of approval. I didn't realize how anxiously I'd been waiting for that. "Anybody crews more than once for Lew, he's either crazy or broke, and you don't look broke."

"He's eased up on me some," Leo said.

"Any special excitement around here lately, Christy?" Sim asked.

"Moonbeam got chased naked all over the docks by a tourist lady with a fish knife, but that's too long a story to tell you now. Billy was the only one saw the whole show."

"Wouldn't he be the one, now?" Marty said sadly.

"The other thing is, Dink beat up on Leo here last Thursday night, and then Lew and Orbie finally took care of Dink. Orbie can tell you better than me. At the end, Dink wouldn't get up when he could have."

"Wisht we'd got around to it first," Sim said. "About time for it. How's Dink acting?"

"Quiet and polite, and we don't see so much of him. Dave acts like it was all a special Christmas present for him alone. One of Gus's daughters was here a while. Charterboat business has been holding up better than anybody thought it would. Orbie gets rid of this batch of girls from the North on Saturday. Everything else is the same. You boys can stop standing on one leg now. I'm through talking. Glad you had a good charter."

"It was the customers made it good, Christy. Three sweet guys. Nobody quarreling, nobody sick, nobody stinking. A lot of laughs. And solid fishing," Marty said. "You never saw bonefishing like we all had on those flats back of Frazier's Hog Cay. They like to come up and chew the tip off the rod, I swear."

"Three good charters in a row," Sim said. "Next time we'll have sorry people and no fish."

"Come on, boy," Marty said. "Those gals are lonesome and the kids are stashed in bed."

"Nice to meet you, Leo."

They turned off into the night toward the parking lot. I heard Sim laugh. It was a young sound, full of joy. My envy, God help me, was like a knife in my heart. Sim, Marty and Jerry were best friends, went through school together, drank and fought and hunted and fished together. We triple-dated together when it was all clear that Sim would marry Gloria and Marty would marry Mary Lee and I'd marry Jerry. When I think of them it's like having your nose flat against cold glass, looking into a warm place full of candy.

"They're nice," Leo said.

"They're both all man," I said as we strolled back toward the reassembled group. "Not all man the way Dink thinks he is. Or even Orbie and Lew. There's a gentle-

95

ness, Leo. Plus the kind of spirit that can't be broken."
I stopped by the old bench in the darkness where I used
to see Jess sitting in the sun, years ago.

"Sit down and let me tell you something that happened
a long time ago to Marty. Sim and Marty were both wild
crazy kids." Leo sat beside me. "Marty was eighteen. He
got interested in Mary Lee. She was, and is, a beauty. A
rough, mean character——he's now up in Raiford for armed
robbery——was interested in Mary Lee, but she wanted no
part of him. The rough type and three of his buddies
cornered Marty one night and took him out behind a
drive-in and gave him a horrible beating. He marked every
one of them, but there were too many. When he was helpless, they picked him up and backed him up against the
building. Two of them held him there. The one that's now
in Raiford, pulled his fist back, saying he was going to
give Marty a face Mary Lee would get sick to her stomach
if she looked at. 'You better kill me,' Marty mumbled.
With his fist still back, the other boy said, 'What you
mean?' Marty lifted his chin off his chest and he stared at
that boy with his one good eye. 'A beating is okay,' he
said. 'I'll take that. But I won't take this.' 'How can you
stop it?' 'I can't. But when I get well, I'm coming after
you. And I'm going to kill every one of you. No matter
where you go. No matter what you do. You do this to
me and I live, you're dead. So you better kill me right now.'

"One of the boys who helped do it told me about
it. He said it changed his whole life right there, with that
one blue eye blazing at him. In a little while the leader
dropped his fist. They let go of Marty and he fell down.
And they walked away fast and left him there and they
didn't mess with him again."

Leo was silent for a long time. Then he said softly,
"The pride and the dignity of the individual. It's the kind
of pride that refuses to accept humiliation. It's that tired
but, damn it, powerful old credo. Better to die on your
feet than live on your knees. It was that same thing in
Marty that caused the Hungarian rebellion, and will make
it happen again one day."

"I agree."

He shifted on the bench. "But suppose you've run out
of pride, Christy? Suppose you had it once, and thought

you still had it, but when you looked you found it had disappeared?"

"I think it's time you talked to me, Leo."

"I—I don't think so."

"If it wasn't time, you wouldn't have said what you just said."

"Maybe I don't want you to see how empty I am."

"I'm glad you're that concerned about what I think."

"I'm suddenly surprised to find out how much I care." His tone became lighter. "Must be something insidious about you."

"I'm insidious, and I'm ravenous. Old Bessie is gassed and ready, and I know a place where they don't care how you're dressed while you eat their big juicy charcoal-broiled steaks."

He drove old Bessie, my shambling Chevrolet. In a weak moment, a year ago, I had her painted shocking pink. She wears this brave hue with the somewhat shame-faced manner of an alley cat wearing a satin bow. When I park her, I half expect her to sidle over to a lamp post and try to rub it off.

I directed him to a steak house nine miles down A-1-A. No music, no tablecloths, no lighting effects, and chipped china a good half inch thick. Sawdust on the floor, and big bandanas for napkins. But the service is fast, the steak tender, the knives sharp, the drinks generous. We had a brace of Martinis while they were broiling our sirloins, an utter lack of conversation after they arrived, sizzling, and then a period of recuperation over a pair of stingers. As though we had made some mutual agreement, the conversation stayed feather-light. We made up signs to put in Bessie's rear window. Our favorite was *Help Stamp Out Togetherness,* which was Leo's contribution.

Once, just after we knocked ourselves out laughing at something or other, he said, "Christy, you're so damn comfortable to be with."

"A good old shoe," I said, unconsciously making one of my faces.

"Stop mugging!" he snapped. "It makes me feel like an audience. When you do that it's like slamming a door in my face."

"I'm sorry," I said. "I just forgot."

"Not an old shoe. That isn't what I mean. I mean the absence of Thurber's war between the sexes."

"I'm neuter?"

"Hardly. And stop twisting my profundities, Miss Yale. I don't have to think before I speak. I find that refreshing. I have the feeling you actually listen when I talk. That too, is refreshing. And when you talk, that zany outlook of yours casts a special illumination on very ordinary things."

"Joe says I have a special awareness for the ridiculous."

"Joe is right. And it does me good, more good than I can tell you, to be out with a young girl and laugh with a young girl."

I looked at him demurely. "Golly, it's so wonderful to bring a little sunshine into the life of such a dear old gramps. Gee whiz, imagine being out with a man old enough to be my father, I mean if you were pretty precocious when you were ten years old. I think it's just so wonderful I didn't have to push your wheelchair in here. And you hardly tremble a bit. I'm glad you made me leave my dolly and my bubblegum out in the car, Gramps."

"Stop it! Stop it!" he said. "I take it back."

"Let's roll it, Father Time."

We drove slowly back. Somehow it had gotten to be eleven, and we marveled at that. Half a moon was doing a dandy silver job on the beach. Even the late neon, in all its candy colors, was pretty. I do not know precisely when his mood changed, when the lightness was gone out of him. But I suddenly realized I was making my jokes to an audience of one. Me. So I subsided.

D Dock had been folded up and put away for the night. There were only the dock lights, and the lights on Sid Stark's boat, and a light on Orbie's *Mine*. If Sid was having a party, it was an intimate one. We paused by the *Shifless* and, conscious of the people sleeping around us, made in soft voices the little awkward sounds of parting. Like saying, "Well . . . well . . . well now."

He said, "I could offer a niggardly amount of bad brandy, what's left in the bottom of the bottle. Or a tepid beer, on account of Billy forgot to bring my ice."

"Myself, I'm a drinking woman," I said, knowing full well that it was just one of those automatic invitations that you make, expecting them to be refused. But I didn't want an end to the evening.

So we walked out toward the end of the dock and went aboard the *Ruthless*. "Odd name for a boat," I said.

"They told me the previous owner bought it to celebrate his divorce."

"Corny name for a boat."

"Then he remarried her."

"And had to sell, of course."

We sat on either side of the small hinged table opposite the galley and sipped the brandy, which was almost as bad as he said it was, out of coffee cups. Things were pretty forced. We'd lost the flavor of the evening. I planned to take off as soon as I could swallow what he'd poured me.

"Another thing, Christy," he said suddenly, and the quality of his voice changed it all back again, back to intimacy.

"What?"

"You don't push. You don't keep digging for the answer to the question you were asking before we left here."

"It doesn't mean I gave up."

"Will you listen? Now?"

"Yes, Leo. Yes."

Suddenly his ugly-nice face twisted into a mask of such special, personal, private agony, that I felt myself the intruder I was.

"The name is not Leo Rice," he said. "It's Leo Harrison."

I wasn't very quick. I guess I stared at him blankly. He had stopped talking and was watching me, so it was supposed to mean something. And suddenly it did. Rigsby and the woman and the suicide. The poor driven bastard. My throat closed up, and tears suddenly ran out of these jack-o-lantern eyes and down this urchin face.

"Oh, my darling!" I whispered.

He stopped looking at me then. He looked down into his empty cup, his arms heavy on the table, and he told me about all of it. The words were narrative—factual and objective as any case history. With the logical quality of his mind, he made it consecutive, not finding it necessary to go back and fill in things he missed. All the emotion was in the timbre of his voice, in the way the words would tumble, and then come one by one, with difficulty. When he had finished—and I had sat so utterly still I felt numbed—there didn't seem to be anything to say.

He looked at me then, and tried to smile. "I was a damn fool. You're wise enough to see that. If I could have been one of those nine to five boys, none of it would have happened. Seven to eleven, six and seven days a week. The big rationalization. I was doing it for her. But I wasn't. I was doing it for myself, to prove I could climb up above the timberline, up into stock-option country, fat bonus country. My picture in trade journals. I advised Congressional committees. I've been mentioned in *Time* and *Newsweek*. Isn't that overwhelming? While I was pumping up my ego, I gradually lost my wife without realizing it was happening. I had made a fallacious evaluation of which part of my life was more important."

"She was ambitious for you?"

"Yes. More so in the beginning. And indifferent at the end."

"So wasn't it her decision too, Leo?"

"In a sense, but I don't want to rationalize that."

"You're very severe with yourself."

"Justifiably, Christy."

I looked at him. A human in misery. I shook my head slowly. "Why did you come down here?"

"Now I don't know. To look at him, talk to him, make him say something about her. And he did. Masochism, maybe. Making the hurt worse. I'm wondering if I can kill him."

"Can you?"

"I don't know. And anything less seems so—damn trivial. Expose myself and cry, I am the husband of the woman you betrayed, sirrah! Put up your hands. A schoolyard sequence at best. Even if I could whip him, which doesn't seem very likely, I can't imagine getting much satisfaction out of it."

"Which is a sign of your maturity."

"Death is less trivial."

"He ought to be put out of circulation, Leo. I'll go along with that. It's a problem any stock breeder would know how to handle."

It startled him. "That's pretty direct."

"Oh, we females are primitive. If you'd ever been captured by Indians, you'd know all about us."

"I want you to understand that I don't blame Lucille. It hurt. I admit that. Had she lived and had I found out about it, I would probably have become a tragic suffering figure. There is no stuffed shirt like the betrayed husband who has been entirely faithful."

"Entirely?"

He smiled. "In deed, if not in thought. I've thought a lot about myself lately, trying to find out what sort of man I am. In all the years of marriage I didn't slip once. And I felt smug about it. And righteous. It is a deviation from the cultural norm."

"Oh, yes indeed."

"Now I know what it was. I felt guilt about how little time I gave my marriage. So I could always say to myself, in excuse, Well I may work till midnight, but at least I haven't done *that* to her."

"Leo, I would have thought that after this happened, you would have just worked harder than before."

"I tried that. But there was no pleasure in accomplishment. None. I finally engineered a ticklish merger, one I'd been struggling with a long time. And when we got S.E.C. approval and the final papers were signed, it didn't mean a thing. All the juice had gone out of it. They think I'm coming back. I won't go back, Christy, no matter what happens. I'll have to go back to clean up personal matters, the house and all, but no more than that."

"Can you just—quit?"

"It won't be a popular decision. There'll be pressure. Financially I can. I've exercised my stock options. It's more growth than income. I could sell out, take my capital gains, and reinvest in income stuff. I've set up a trust for the boys. I can live carefully. But I can't go back to that. Every day I'd be totally aware of what it had cost me. You see, she wasn't a weak woman, Christy. But she wasn't one of those women who can divert all her warmth toward her kids. A man's woman. And I gutted her. I deprived her of the most valid reason for her existence. So she was restless and searching for something she couldn't name. Vulnerable as hell. So Rigsby took away from her the only thing she had left—pride

101

and dignity. He killed her. And I don't think I can return the favor."

And he began to break. Part of it was the reaction to telling me. His face began to come apart. Sometimes there have to be arms around you. I slid quickly around and gave him the arms he needed. I pulled his head into the hollow of my throat, made comforting noises. The sob of an adult male can be grotesque comedy. Red Skelton uses it sometimes. But the sob of a strong man, with a reason to sob, is a thing that can shake you all the way down to the cellar of your heart.

He had one arm around me as I held him. And his arm was strong. There were two lights on. I was able to reach up and click off the stronger one. I wanted all his unshed tears. I wanted to be a great deep pillow for his grief. I felt him fighting it, and wished he wouldn't, but knew it was part of him to fight it. When he sat up again, I didn't want him to go. His arm was still around me, and he put his mouth down upon mine, upon this clown mouth, this girl and a half mouth, in tenderness, in gratitude. But it lasted just long enough so that something else was added to it.

He kissed me again, and it was mostly something else, his mouth hardening as mine softened, with breathing quickening and my arms growing strong as I tried to curve myself against him as close as I wanted to be, and could not manage in that cramped little space, where the edge of the table cut sharply into my waist. It became a little blindness for us, groping and gasping, bruising our lips.

He released me abruptly and we moved apart like guilty children. "I didn't plan anything like that," he said, looking at me with a perturbing wonder.

"Oh, I cooked it all up, dear," I said. "When you told me you were rich, I couldn't help myself."

His smile was slow. "And I know better than that, too."

"I can make some phrases. What could we have been thinking of? It shall never happen again, sir. We were carried away by proximity. We must control ourselves. It was the animal in us, Gramps. And I better go home."

"The last phrase is the good one," he said. "Get me aroused and no telling how bestial I might become."

I stood up in the narrow aisle. He got up behind me. I

started to put one foot on the two steps that would take me topside. And suddenly there was a bold explosion in my heart. I turned and looked at him. I felt as if my hands were the size of bait pails and I didn't know what to do with them. The dim light helped.

"Leo . . ." I said, my voice more of a croak than usual.

"What is it?"

"I'm all it?"

"I'm all hoyden all of a sudden. A bawd. A loose wench. Leo, no claims, no recriminations. I swear. Cross my heart. I mean if you could want to, I want to." I was prattling and I couldn't stop. "I'm terribly out of practice, and my underwear is mended, but it's span clean. We can make out like it never happened, if we try, but I want a chance to make out like it never happened. And before I can do that, it has to happen, doesn't it."

"If I could want to!" he said. "Good God! It isn't that, but I don't—"

So I rushed him. I ran thump into his chest and found his mouth with mine at the first plunge. I nearly dropped him onto his back. Christy, the demure type. I found I could fit against him much more pleasantly than in the booth but by then, of course, that much closeness wasn't enough either. After we got into the forward cabin I started prattling again, my voice squeaking with nervousness, saying how it was a tiresome thing for a girl who wanted to be slipping sleekly out of silks and laces to have to struggle with a dang pair of bluejean shorts and an old yellow T shirt which I adored even though I know yellow is the wrong color for me, because it makes me look sort of green in the face, and . . .

He put a firm and gentle hand over my mouth and when he took it away, I could keep from talking. He helped me off with what my shaking hands hadn't been able to manage. He got me into the bunk and I was shivering, and I got a twitch in the muscle of the calf of my right leg so that the whole leg kept leaping about like a mackerel in the bottom of a skiff. Christy, the great courtesan. He held me gently and patiently until the shivering stopped and the little motor in my leg ran down. Then he kissed me.

I don't know how it was. I've got the weirdest sort of memory. I know the lyrics of a hundred songs, and a lot of them are not terribly nice, but what else goes with my laryngical croak? I can remember the pictures in my first reader, clear as clear. But when the big things happen, my mind seems to be turned off.

I do know that for a while it was two living things. And it became one entity, with no more thee and me, or thine and mine. And it had the feeling of being *meant* to be that way, as if there was something forlorn and drab about being just one separate thing by yourself all alone. And I felt that all of me had been combined. All the layers of self, so separate, were stirred into one broth, and so I was able to be present at that time and place in a way I had never been present before. A supra-awareness, and good because all the selves were for giving, not taking.

I can't avoid using some of those silly, overworked, sappy words. So I have to say some of it was tender and some of it was savage, some of it was sweet and some of it was fierce as growling.

I am supposed to have a good imagination. And I've read the analogies they write where they compare the end of it to the sea, or music or fireworks or the earth shaking and so on. But it wasn't like that. I felt proud that it was so good, and then it became better and then it became incredibly better, and when I knew there was no enduring it, it suddenly swooped up so high that I was beyond any place where I could sort out comparisons about the sea and aerial bombs and so on. It was just a gigantic, indescribable, prolonged *something* that was happening to me, so important that I didn't even know my own name, or what I was, or where I was.

But my memory of the mechanics is utterly blank.

I didn't really crawl all the way back into my own skin until we lay side by side, my head on his arm, my heart slowing to an easy canter. I felt unbearably smug. In kindergarten, when you were very good, they would send you home with a gold star stuck on your forehead. I wanted one of those.

"Christy, Christy, Christy," he whispered.

"I know. Don't talk. I just want to feel like this. Like a lump of butter. Golly."

In a little while I opened my eyes and lifted my head a little. The moon had moved. It came down through the oblong portholes and made one patch on my breasts and another on his hairy knees, both patterns of light moving slightly with the tiny shifting of the *Ruthless* at her mooring.

I hoped he was looking at me. They're the best of me, I think. I looked at him and couldn't see where he was looking. Our heads were in darkness.

So suddenly it startled me, he grabbed me and slid me down until my face was in moonlight. He braced himself up on one elbow and said, "You're beautiful, Christy."

I covered my face with my hands. He took my two wrists in his hand and pulled my hands away and said, "I mean it."

Old leaky-eye Christy. I snuffled and said, "I knew nobody was ever going to say that again."

"Whoever says it sees what I see. And it's not hard to see. Not obscure at all."

"I better look again."

He kissed the wet eyes. "Oh, Christy."

"Just you remember it was my idea, hear?"

"I wonder just how good the idea was?"

"What?"

"Don't snarl at me. I meant—biologically."

"Oh," I said dreamily. "Oh, that."

"Don't you think you should—"

"Uh-uh. I'm too comfortable."

"But Christy!"

"Somehow I don't care. He'll be born smiling."

He lay back. "Okay, okay, horrify the Chamber of Commerce. How big are those brothers?"

"Monsters, every one. Short tempers, too. Very protective."

"And conservative?"

"Highly."

He held my hand. I felt nifty. Without particular thought, I said dreamily, "I guess I'll have you marry me anyway."

Suddenly he was laughing so hard he shook the bunk. I sat up and said, "What's so hilarious, old buddy?"

When he could speak he said, "I just remembered . . . what you said. About no . . . claims. Wow!"

I tried to hang onto my annoyance, but I couldn't. I knew how crazy it had sounded. But, damn it, when you feel smug, you sound smug. So I helped him laugh it up.

Later he put the palm of his hand on my tummy. Just

as I was hoping that he appreciated its hard-won flatness, several thousand sneaky little electric worms began to hurry all over me, traveling just under the skin. I felt as if any minute I would start to glow bright blue. I gulped, spun toward him, and tried to dig a hole in his chest. And I remember even less about our second production. But I do remember thinking, just as the world began to become too immediate to think about, that it was going to play hell if from now on any little touch activated those thousand-watt worms. I'd spend most of my declining years in a state of semi-consciousness and brisk abandon.

When I met him on the dock the next day at five thirty, I suddenly felt, standing there in the sunlight, as if I had been issued an undersized fig leaf. I wanted to hide under a bait bucket. Then he smiled, and I wanted to sling him over my shoulder and gallop to my cave with him. He explained why it had been essential to phone me eleven times at the C of C. Just to say hello, of course. I explained the little bruise over my eye. I had walked into a window wall. I said let's go swimming first. He didn't have to ask before what. I always say an intelligent girl never, never makes herself too available. That's what I always say. But what if you've fallen way behind, because he took so long to show up in your life, and, without being egocentric, only smug, you feel you have uncovered a rare natural talent? What about that?

TEN

Happy Birthday

THE YEAR AFTER JESS DIED, the citizens of Stebbins' Marina gave a surprise birthday party for Alice. It was a genuine surprise that first year. And almost a surprise the second year. By the third year it was a tradition.

As with all new traditions, it takes a few years to make all the necessary adjustments. It was decided that the celebration of her fifty-first birthday would be the biggest, best and smoothest yet. Though it was still called a surprise birthday party, no attempt was made to conceal the preparations from Alice.

On Friday some men from an awning company came and put up a big rental tent—a gaudy three-sided affair—in the open space between the shower buildings and the big apron which ran along the shoreside end of all four docks. A big trestle table was set up in the tent as a bar. Men from a lighting outfit came with all the floodlights the dock wiring system could handle and set them securely in place where they were least likely to be damaged.

It had been learned that the combination of the dimness of the docks and the spirit of holiday had been, in a few instances in the past, unfortunate. The expenses of the tent and the wiring, the kegs of beer, the bartenders, the rental glasses, and a stupendous quantity of cold buffet, to be doled out a banquet at a time, were guaranteed by the permanent residents. For the last four years the investors had made a profit. Half the profit, by tradition, went to buy a present for Alice, and the rest went into a closed party a week later, a party by invitation only.

Everyone who knew about the party—and who had

five bucks—could come. Your ticket was the five dollar bill. In return the back of your hand was firmly stamped with indelible ink. In return for your five dollars, you were entitled to all the beer you could drink, at a nickel a glass, provided you brought the glass back to be refilled. If you didn't, your next beer cost you two bits, and you took better care of your glass.

On previous years Helen Hass had proved she was the person to handle the money. She did not drink. She would spend the afternoon and evening going back and forth through the crowd at a slow trot, bent forward from the waist, looking for unstamped hands and collecting money to shove into the office safe.

If you refused to pay, some muscular charterboat operators would grab your arms, run you all the way to the edge of the parking lot, and see how much elevation they could give you. Lew Burgoyne and Sim Gallowell held the record, having, in 1957, cleared three sedans with one cooperative heave of a rather small drunk. Only the most stout of heart returned after such a definitive dismissal.

The other way to leave violently was to pay your money and then behave outrageously. But such were the standards of behavior that to be so treated was a rarity and considered a distinction. A plump little tourist man achieved that honor in 1956 when he solemnly set the tent on fire. They threw him into the lot three times before he made it known that he merely wanted to get back to his boat over at B Dock and go to bed. So they threw him onto his boat.

Paying customers were also entitled to partake of the buffet, join the 'talent' show, fall off the docks as they saw fit, get thunderously drunk, beat each other's faces in, pursue members of the opposite sex with all the vigor at their command, sing, belly-dance, roar at the moon, and fall down unconscious.

If you had no taste for beer, you could bring your own bottle, hand it over to the bartender with your name on it, and buy it back, with setups, at two bits a paper cup. Or you could keep it on your boat, or a friend's boat.

It had become larger each year. As this one fell on a Saturday night, it was anticipated that it would be the biggest yet. All tourist craft were warned that if they valued their lives, their night's rest, and the honor of their womenfolk, it would be wise to find another anchorage.

The police cooperated by staying away.

Perhaps the wide popularity of the birthday party was in part due to the time of year. The hot months bring tensions and a flavor of potential violence. This was release.

One change had been made this year. Instead of using an area at the neck of one of the docks for the talent show, Sid Stark had offered the rear deck of his big Chris. It was a flush rear deck, high over the dock. He had an elaborate high-fidelity system aboard. He had a technician come out and rent him a floor microphone and what other electronic gadgets he needed to tie it into his big speakers, which were moved up to the flying bridge. Special spots were rigged to illuminate the improvised stage, and everybody agreed that it was a splendid innovation. It was obvious that a few people might get accidentally pushed off D Dock, but it was wide enough to hold a throng, and besides you could see the stage clearly from shore.

It was expected that this year some of Sid's friends from the entertainment world would add a more professional flair to the program. And it was hoped there would be fewer amateur strippers. When the show was over, Sid's tapes would provide the music for the fiesta.

Because it was Saturday, the official starting time was pushed forward to three o'clock, thus guaranteeing that there would be a certain almost predictable percentage who would miss seeing the shades of night.

Billy Looby spent the week readying his 'gallery.' Men only. No children. That stipulation was redundant. Children were not permitted at the party. No one wanted the responsibility for warping little minds. The walls of Billy's room in the end of the storage shed were papered with such intemperate examples of pornography, most of it from Havana, that strong men had been known to stop dead just inside the door, gasp and look sickly. It was Billy's hobby, and he arranged them in as telling a way as possible, determined to see that no man felt cheated by his fifty cents admission fee.

On Friday morning, at high tide, a Texas yacht out of Galveston inched cautiously into the basin. It was as big

109

as anything that had ever stopped there, a little over a hundred feet of converted Canadian cutter, named *Do Tell*. The only place for it was alongside the T at the end of D Dock. The yacht was bright and smart, the crew brisk in uniform. Alice looked it up in Lloyds and found, as she suspected, that it was corporate owned.

She went out and told them what they might be getting into. She guessed there were perhaps two dozen people aboard, a lot of sun-brown, slow-talking men, the majority of them in their middle years, and a smaller number of leggy girls, all of them young. A lament of the wide prairree played softly over the yacht's speaker system.

The men and young girls lounged on the decks with tall drinks and one of the men said, "Ma'am, this is just plain fool luck, that's all. Never yet run from a party and we're not about to start. I'd say no matter how rough it gets, we've seen rougher one time or another."

On Saturday only the *Bally-Hey* and the *Jimmy-Jan* went out on a half-day charter. All day charters were, for once, refused. During the early part of the day a dozen cruisers and fishing boats from marinas up and down the Waterway moved into the basin and tied up at the places Billy Looby found for them. This was too good to miss. If it lived up to other years, it would provide local conversation for months. As the basin became more crowded, the feeling of expectancy increased.

The committee, this year, had consisted of Gus Andorian, Helen Hass, Joe Rykler, Amy Penworthy and Orbie Derr. They had all worked hard, except Joe. He had been worse than useless, forgetting to do the few things that Helen, the chairman, had given him to do. In Joe's emotional absence, occasioned by his very obvious, very intense and very unsuccessful pursuit of Anne Browder, Lew Burgoyne had filled in.

At one o'clock, two hours before the official time of the opening of the party, the committee met on Gus's old *Queen Bee*.

"It won't rain," Orbie said firmly. "I got the noon report out of Miami."

"Wonderful," Helen said.

"And," Orbie continued, "I got those eight Bitty-Beddy

110

girls on the eleven o'clock plane and that's more wonderful. Yelping like hound dogs, they were, about missing the party. But, by God, can you figure how it would be, me running around trying to keep 'em out of trouble in a party like this one is going to be? Man! It half sickens me to think on it. And that's the last damn batch this year. I'm howling tonight."

"The main thing is, have we got enough beer and food?" Amy said. They stared at each other, wearing slight frowns.

"Not enough," Gus said gloomily.

They had discussed it many times, and had finally ended up ordering twenty-five per cent more of everything than on the previous year.

"That isn't the main thing at all," Helen said in her most crisp executive manner. "The main thing is to keep it from getting too rough. Are you all set on that, Lew?"

A big white grin showed in the middle of his corsair beard. "I'm staying close to sober, cutie, and so are five buddies."

"How close?"

"Not so close we won't have no fun at all, but not so far we won't be able to put the lid on fast if we have to. We're going to keep circulating every minute."

She studied him for a moment and then nodded. "There's not much else we can do. They should be arriving with the stuff pretty soon. The tent is ready. I'll be taking money and using the stamp. All we can do is hope it's a nice party. Amy, how about the talent show?"

"We decided eight o'clock, Helen. A friend of Sid's is going to be the M.C. Sid says he's worked in big places. He says he's real funny. Eight o'clock should be about right. He'll have a sort of a program I made out."

"Is Christy going to sing?"

Orbic answered, "We had a terrible time talking her into it. Told her how well it went over last year and all, and how much Alice liked it. She just didn't want to, but finally she said okay. She and me though, only rehearsed one time. I never seen a girl change so much so fast, I swear."

"Love," Amy explained with a sigh.

"She wants to sing straight," Orbie said worriedly. "A

111

couple ballads. I don't know how it'll go over, I honest to God don't. I guess Leo is all right, but . . ."

"Well, I guess we're all set," Helen said. "You've been a very good committee."

There was almost a concerted sigh. Soon it would be out of their hands. It was as if they had drilled holes in a rocky cliff, planted the charges and lit the fuse. Now all they could do would be watch it go off.

"Anybody think of any special problems?" Helen asked, standing up.

"Moonbeam could get to be one," Lew said. "If Captain Jimmy should figure on passing out too early. I mean if she sets up in business too obvious, it might not go so good with the womenfolk."

"You see if you can keep Captain Jimmy slowed down some," Orbie said.

"Sure thing."

"Lew," Helen said, "you remember to have one of your boys take a look once in a while to make sure they're staying off the boats in storage."

"Sure thing."

The committee meeting broke up. They filed off Gus's boat, looking more worried than festive. Orbie motioned to Lew, and Lew followed him out to the *Mine* and went aboard with him into the neat, gleaming, air-conditioned orderliness of the main cabin of the houseboat.

"Sit down," Orbie said. "We could get us a small start with one beer."

"Couldn't hurt a thing. Don't mind if I do."

Orbie opened the beers. They took deep swallows.

"Got a minute?" Orbie asked.

"All you need."

"I didn't want to bring this up in front of the others. Fact is, I'm going back on my word even telling you. But I figure it's another place where there could be trouble and you ought to know about it so you can keep an eye on it."

"What's this all about?"

"I've known Christy a long time, almost as long as Sim and Marty's known her. She's all gal."

"I go along with that. Couple of times I made a pass at her, damn if she didn't get me laughing so hard I forgot

112

what I was after."

"Same here, Lew. What do you think about her and this Leo Rice?"

Burgoyne pursed his lips and knuckled his beard. "Well, all of a sudden they're in love so hard it gives me the itch to see them together. It sure was fast and complete. You asking me if it's a good thing? Hell, I don't know. I've got so I like him pretty good. I wisht he wouldn't talk so careful. But you take the way I worked him and the way he kept getting up so Dink could knock him down, he's got a good gravel bottom. He don't scare, and he learns quick. Hell, Orbie, why shouldn't he learn quick? You know he's a big shot businessman. Plenty of money. He don't look the kind to go knocking a woman around. Christy must be thirty.

"I guess what I think about her and Leo—I guess I think it's a good thing for her. I mean I never heard of her messing around any, and I guess it's just as unnatural for a gal as it is for a man to go too many years without any sack time at all.

"Now don't you get that scowly look, Orbie. I'm not badmouthing Christy and you know it. I don't want to have to go round and round with you and get all wore out for the party. I'm thinking the whole thing out as I go along. Anybody can see, from the way they just look at each other, they can't hardly wait to get alone again. And, by God, it makes me feel sorta lonesome, as if I'm missing out by nobody looking at me like that. Yes, I guess it's a good thing, all the way around."

"So what if he hurts her by just taking off?"

"I don't think he's the kind of a guy who'd . . ." Lew stopped abruptly and clenched a big brown scarred fist. "Say, you don't mean that son of a bitch was lying about his wife being dead, do you? If he's pulled that, I'm going to take him by the—"

"Slow down, for God's sake. Nothing like that. Christy come to me for advice. Or maybe just to talk it out. It helps you with your own thinking if you talk things out. His wife is dead. She kilt herself last year. Rice isn't his name. She didn't tell me his real name. He came here on purpose, to get a good close look at Rigsby. She took a vacation in Nassau and got messed up with Rigsby and

113

he raised such pure hell with her before he kicked her off the ketch, she kilt herself."

Lew stared at him, wide-eyed. "God damn!"

"Now this is secret and private, Lew. I shouldn't be telling you. Christy has been trying to talk Leo out of doing anything stupid. She told me she's been telling him that now they found each other, it makes everything different. But it doesn't make it different enough, I guess. He's enough man so that even if he has got a new woman, that doesn't cancel out why he come here."

"To kill him?"

"Maybe. She doesn't know and I don't know, and I don't think Leo is too clear about it in his mind. But he just can't go away with Christy and spend the rest of his life thinking about what he maybe should have done."

"I've sure wondered why he was giving Rigsby the time of day."

"She told me he got Rigsby to talk about the woman that kilt herself. She said it was a pretty spooky type thing."

"Hell, yes."

"I can remember just about exactly how Christy put it to me. She said she was scared. She said she's found her guy, but now she's afraid she might all of a sudden lose him because there's one part of him she can't reach. That's the part about Rigsby. She says he's getting more tensed up all the time. She's afraid if he gets a little tight at the party, something is going to blow. And he don't stand a chance in hell of beating Rigsby up. Hell, that time you and Rigsby met up nose to nose, it took you damn near an hour to lick him, and after you did, he wasn't as chopped up as you were."

"I don't know. I was just fun-fighting. It's different when a man has a reason big as the one Leo has. My, I'd like to watch that fight."

"If we could be sure that's all it would be, okay. Leo would get it out of his system, providing he didn't get clobbered too fast. But maybe he'll get a club or a gun and kill him like you kill a snake. And ruin everything for him and Christy. She shouldn't be hurt bad again. You know that."

"I know that. Yes."

"Rigsby's leaving day after tomorrow, and Leo knows

114

that too. That's why she figures he might make his move tonight. And she doesn't know what it will be. She can't get him to talk about it or promise he won't do anything. You and me, boy, we better stay close as we can in case it looks like a good idea to bust something up."

"We can take turns, like."

"All right. But don't you let on to Christy I told you all this, or we will have to go round and round."

Lew grinned and closed his right hand effortlessly, crushing the empty beer can. "Let's do that anyway, again some time. Been over a year. Just a little fun-fighting, Orbie. Stand-up, stuff, with no stomping and no gouging."

"Next week, maybe, if I feel real good."

Lew started out. He turned back and said, "You hear about Rigsby snufflin' around Judy Engly?"

"Everybody knows that but Jack."

"He make out yet?"

Orbie shrugged. "I'd say maybe no. Alice chewed her last week for having anything to do with him. She went all sulky and told Alice she wasn't doing anything wrong, and what business was it of hers?"

"Now Jack could lick him for sure."

"For surely sure."

Lew left the houseboat, slowly and thoughtfully.

By two o'clock, an hour before post time, the party began to stir. It made its first evidence on the moored cruisers. Stan and Beezie Hooper, with several house guests, came down to the marina and started a small social gathering aboard the *Fleetermouse,* airing it out, opening the ports, setting out the chairs and rubber mattresses, setting up a self-service bar, and getting Billy Looby to bring out a supply of ice. Billy, as on previous years, had stocked a monster supply of ice in blocks and cubes—and raised the price.

This year he had improved the range of his service by laying in two cases of cheap bourbon and two cases of cheap gin. With each ice delivery to a boat he would wink and say, "Iffen you folks should run out of drinkin' liquor . . ."

The breeze died. The high white sun leaned its tropic weight on the gaudy vacation strip of Florida's East

Coast, so that it lay sunstruck, lazy and humid and garish, like a long brown sweaty woman stretched out in sequins and costume jewelry. The sun baked the sand too hot for tourist feet. Slow swells clumped onto the listless Atlantic beach. The sun turned road tar to goo, overheated the filtered water in the big swimming pools of the rich and the algaed pools of the do-it-yourself clan, blazed on white roofs, strained air conditioners, turned parked cars into tin ovens, and blistered the unwary. A million empty roadside beer cans twinkled in the bright glare. The burning heat dropped a predictable number of people onto stone sidewalks, of which a predictable number died, drove the unstable further into the jungly wastes of their madness, exposed the pink tongues of all the dogs in the area, redoubled the insect songs in every vacant lot, set the weather-bureau boys to checking the statistics of past performance, and sent a billion billion salty trickles to flowing on sin-darkened skins.

At the Stebbins' Marina, all exposed metal was too hot to touch. No one stayed below, except on the air-conditioned boats. The small boat traffic, back and forth from the basin entrance to A Dock, had a sleepy, buzzing sound about it, deadened by the hot mugginess of the air. Only the brownest and toughest ones stretched themselves out to endure the predictable agony of the sun. There was a dazed jumble of music, much of it Cuban, from boat radios and record players. Tall tinkling drinks turned tepid the moment the last sliver of ice disappeared.

At three-thirty, half an hour after the bar in the tent opened, Helen Hass made her first deposit in the office safe. She had toured the whole basin with her rubber stamp, ink pad, small counting machine and dark-eyed diligence. Each time she stamped a hand, she clicked the counter.

She pushed dark hair back off her damp forehead with the back of her hand, sat at the desk and counted the first batch. She had also caught some of the early arrivals who had come by car. Soon the lot would be full. A little over seven hundred dollars. It checked out. She put it in the safe and spun the dial.

Alice came heavily down the stairs. "Hi, Helen. That darn little window conditioner up there is making it hotter, seems like."

"It's terrible!"

"Getting any customers?"

"Not too many yet. They're in the shade, drinking beer."

"Don't you work too hard, honey, in this heat. Suppose some do sneak in and don't pay, does it matter much?"

"It does to me!"

"All right, all right. Guess I'll go out and circulate a little. How do I look?"

"Wonderful!" Helen said. It would have been more accurate to say Alice Stebbins looked different. Her standard costume was blue jeans, a pair of raggedy sneakers, a man's white shirt with the collar open and the sleeves rolled high on her brown muscular arms. In the cold months she added a bulky maroon cardigan. In honor of the day she now wore a sheer white feminine blouse, a yellow skirt and high heels. Somehow it made her look older, heavier, rather drab and dull and ordinary.

"Is anything wrong?" Helen asked.

"Why do you ask, honey?"

"I thought you seem sort of . . . listless."

"Just the heat." They stepped out together into the yellow furnace. Three men were heading from the lot toward the docks. Helen darted out and stamped them and got their money.

At about quarter to four Leo Rice, in seersucker robe, carrying his toilet kit, started toward shore. Joe Rykler, lounging alone in the shade of the cockpit of the *Ampersand* said, "Whoa, friend."

"For what?"

"A little stimulator. Does wonders for the endurance. Only takes a moment."

Leo waited. It did not take long. Joe handed him up a small fat pewter mug, misted on the outside. "Thanks, but what is it?"

"A poor thing, but mine own. It's a Marterror. That's what you get when you start to make a Martini and make it too big."

Leo looked at the mug dubiously. "Little early to blast off, isn't it?"

"My first one didn't harm me a bit. Carry it along, old boy. Nurse it, if it alarms you. Just return the mug."

"You look a little blurred around the edges, Joe."

117

"It's my leaky old heart that's blurred around the edges, Leo. She utterly refuses to admit I'm unique, charming, loveable, tender, imaginative, sensitive, manly and indispensable. The woman is a fool. I can make no deal, on any terms, up to and including Platonic marriage, if that's what she wants. Best legs in the whole Congressional district."

"Keep trying. I'll nurse this thing. Carefully."

After Leo walked into the men's shower room, he took an icy gulp of the Marterror and put the mug on the window sill. He took a long shower and another gulp, dried himself and gulped again, and had a few more gulps while he shaved. He was surprised when the final sliver of ice slid up the inside of the empty mug and clicked against his teeth.

He checked himself in the bleary mirror near the urinals, bulging his chest and shoulders, sucking his belly deep as he could. A hell of a drastic change from all that executive type flab, those old rolls of suet. "Fine figger of a man," he muttered, and then grinned at himself in a shamefaced way. But, oh, so much better for all this that was happening with Christy than the way it had been before. Like preparing a gift for her without knowing that was what he was doing. Lean and brown for her. Strong for her. But he had been doing it for Rigsby. Getting ready for Rex. Then doing nothing about it. Delaying the inevitable. But you can't delay it much longer and still live with yourself, or with anybody else. Or shave this face again.

When he put the robe back on and went out into the sunshine the world had that particularly vivid look which made it clear to him that Joe's one Marterror had gotten to him. A lot more people had arrived. The slanting sun was not as vicious. The place was beginning to teem and ferment. The natives were restless.

He stood for a moment outside the shower room, looking at the idiot range of color and costume. Two men in swim trunks, straw sandals and coolie hats. Some men in crisp khakis, bleached almost white. A man in a cord business suit, with a violent tie. A girl in a white dress, with red hat, shoes and purse. A bulbous, barefoot, bleary old female type, in purple slacks and an orange shirt and

118

gold hoop earrings. A stunning girl in a white strapless swim suit, laughing with a less happily endowed girl friend in a cotton sunback dress.

The people from the boats were beginning to mill around with the crowd. Sweating bartenders drew beer in the hot shade of the striped tent, handing it out to the three-deep crowd. Two girls in waitress uniforms were setting up the first installment of the buffet. Cars were parked thick in the lot and along the boulevard. Sid Stark had cut in his special music installation. The hi was very fi, and the tempo was tirelessly jump. Women laughed, showing their teeth and arching their backs. Already great exponents of comedy were slyly spilling dabs of icy beer on the bare feet of the unsuspecting.

As he started back out D Dock there was a gust out of the east, and then the beginnings of a gentle steady breeze. The entire east coast raised its elbows and said, Aaahh.

Just as he reached Joe's boat, he saw Jannifer Jean standing on D Dock by the stern of Sid's *Pieces of Seven*. Captain Jimmy was with her. And a group of males, some familiar to Leo, some not. Moonbeam attracted no sidelong looks or stolen glances. The group of awestruck men had braced their feet, faced her squarely, and were boggling at her. She had evidently fashioned her own Bikini, using three blue bandanas, knotted rather than sewn. The final touch was added by silver sandals with extremely high plastic heels. There seemed to be an almost alarming amount of Jannifer Jean. She was as improbable as any calendar. It brought Leo to a sudden stop.

Joe stepped up onto the dock, took Leo's mug and handed him a full one, and said, "Hold any self-respecting asp to that bosom and it would call for help."

Leo took a gulp of the new drink and said, "Captain Jimmy looks like the little gray duck who hatched the ostrich egg." He looked down at the mug. "Hey! I didn't want this."

"You're committed now, old buddy. Take it along and . . ."

"I know. Nurse it and return the mug."

"Look!" Joe said.

Leo looked back at Moonbeam just in time to see one of her circle of admirers ease up behind her while Captain

Jimmy was engaged in conversation and give one decisive and strategic tug at the blue knot between her sallow shoulder blades. Moonbeam's reaction time was dim. The fabric fell to the dock. She looked stupidly down at it.

Captain Jimmy turned and saw his unencumbered bride, yelped and pounced toward the bandana halter, snatched it up and thrust it at her. Moonbeam took it and held it, turning it this way and that, trying to figure out how it should go. Captain Jimmy was trying to keep himself between her and avid eyes. But as the spectators were standing in a half circle, he was a very busy man. At last she held it against her. Captain Jimy did the knot job. And he made of it a rock-hard knot the size of a hazel nut. As he stepped back from her, one of the spectators turned dreamily away and walked off the dock.

Orbie Derr appeared beside Leo and said, "Looks like things getting off to a good fast start this year."

Leo walked out to the *Ruthless*. The breeze made it bearable below. He put on a dark gray sports shirt and linen shorts in a natural shade, plaid canvas shoes with rope soles. By that time he had nibbled his way through three quarters of his second Marterror.

He walked to the *Shifless*, stepped down onto the stern deck, knocked at the curtained cabin door and heard Christy call, "Just a minute! Who is it?"

"Reo Lice," he called, deliberately spoonerizing his assumed name.

A few moments later she swung the door open and stared round-eyed at him and at the pewter mug.

"One of those things Joe makes! Golly!"

"Everything is looking vivid, darling."

"You're starting mighty early, stranger. Come on in."

"Need anything zipped or snapped, I hope?"

"No thanks. I just hope you'll last."

"I might. Joe won't."

She sat with her back to him, brushing her short hair, scowling at herself in the mirror. He liked the neatness and straightness of her back, the warm line from the narrow waist to the swell of her hips.

"I feel overdressed," she complained.

"That can be rectified."

"You hush up. I have to sing for the people, damn it.

120

Maybe I ought to dress simple now and change later."

"Happy to assist."

She turned and looked at him. "Leo, you are tight already!"

"Got serious objections?"

"No. No objections. Are you going to get tighter?"

"Could be. Can't tell."

She sighed and got up. She went and pulled the curtains more carefully over the windows. She locked the door. "Helen will be too busy to come back here," she said thoughtfully. She strolled slowly toward him, swinging her hips. "It's times like these," she said as he reached for her, "a girl has to think of practically everything." And they clung together, with the clatter of the elderly air conditioning unit drowning out all but the most spectacular sounds of the growing party.

At the same time, Joe Rykler and Marty Urban were dealing with a highly indignant Billy Looby. With an emphatic spray of spittle, Billy was yelling, "You two cheats come pushing and shoving in here and not paying the fifty cents and I—"

"Hush, you dirty little old man," Joe said. "We're the inspection committee. We've got to see if your collection is worth fifty cents a look. If it is, we'll promote it. You'll make millions. What do you think, Marty?"

Marty stood staring at one photograph at eye level, "My, my, my," he said, shaking his head. "The things some folks do for a living."

Joe went over and looked at what had caught Marty's fancy. "Hooooweee," he said faintly.

"And that sweet little smile on her purty little face," Marty said. "By God, Billy, where do you get this junk?"

"I got friends," Billy said proudly. "You fellas could give me one fifty cents. You know, cut price."

"Hey, Marty, look at this one," Joe said.

"Hell, that looks like Moonbeam, only cleaner."

That started them trying to find people in the photographs who looked like people they both knew.

The game came to an abrupt end when Marty, over in a corner, said, "Now this here one has got a built like that leggy Anne Browder you're so hot on."

Joe turned white and said, "How would you like it if

121

I point out one that looks like your Mary Lee?"

Marty whirled. "You do that and I'll plain kill you. It isn't the same." His eyes were narrow.

"To me," Joe said, "it is exactly the same. Maybe you didn't understand that before."

Marty looked sheepish. "Hell, I'm sorry. I'm sorry all to hell, Joey. I shouldn'ta said a thing like that." He set his half glass of beer carefully on the floor, locked his hands behind him and said, sticking his jaw out, "Take a free swing." He closed his eyes. "Come on. I'll feel better."

Joe put his empty mug down and swung. Marty bounced off the wall with a thud that shook the shed, landed on his hands and knees, shook his head violently, spat blood and then grinned up at Joe and said, "Man, you got no more punch than Mary Lee. You're plain pathetic."

"So give me another."

Marty got up and picked up his beer. "There doesn't one of 'em look a bit like Anne. Not a bit."

"She makes them all look like dogs."

"Sure does."

As they strolled out, Billy trotted after them, saying, "You goin' to tell around how good it is this year, with the new stuff I got?"

Joe shook his head sadly, "It isn't anywhere near as good as last year, Billy."

"We couldn't rightly recommend it," Marty said. "I'm sorry all to hell."

"Look at all the new customers!" Joe said.

"What'll we do now?"

"I'm going to switch to beer, to extend my effectiveness over a few more hours, and then go boat-hopping. Come on."

"I better go hunt up Mary Lee afore she goes weasel-eyed on me. Anyhow I see enough of boats all day long to last me."

Rex Rigsby, in a white mesh shirt and pale blue shorts that set off the dark tone of his thick muscular legs, stood apart from the throng in the shade of a storage shed, sipping a Scotch and water and watching the younger women, assaying, with the cool appraisal of the expert, the merit of a golden thigh, the telling sensuousness of a mouth, the tilt and texture of a breast.

When they were aware of him, he was immediately aware of their awareness and could then index them on the basis of age, income level, probable experience and the ease or difficulty of acquisition—much like a cattleman at a stock show making an educated guess as to a specified blood line and placing his bid by a deft signal with pipe or program. He saw nothing he could not index, nothing that could possibly astonish him.

When he finally saw what he had been waiting for, he felt a strengthening of the pulse in his throat, felt his neck and shoulders bulge. She was strolling toward the tent with her husband, Jack Engly. He was holding her hand. Judy wore a rather prim little outfit, a yellow blouse and white skirt, with a wide shiny cheap-looking green belt.

This particular magic had happened to him many times before. He could see her flaws readily—the too-round childish face, rather dull and sulky, her plump, long-waisted, short-legged build, with too much width of hip and sturdiness of thigh and calf, the suggestion of a double chin, the thick stubby hands, the pigeon-fullness of her breast—but even her flaws excited him. He knew that even without the evidence of the wild night-howling that her rangy young husband could so readily induce, he would have known she was one of that rare minority, a woman so deeply and blindly sensuous that little else in life had any meaning to her. With those few, their special dedication is an almost visible aura, a plangent musk, a textured pungency.

But she was being far more difficult than he had expected her to be. She now knew what he was after, and even though there was a provocative air of willingness about her, she had sidestepped all his careful arrangings thus far. When he had been with her over at the public beach, her conversation had been so crashingly inane that it had almost cooled him off. "So that's what you think." "So it's a free world, ain't it?" "Geez, Rex, you say crazy things, hones'." But when the brown eyes looked directly at him, feral and aware, they spoke a private language, making unthinkable promises.

He looked closely at Jack Engly. The big young man

wore a slightly stupefied grin, and he ambled along with the looseness and carelessness of several drinks. Rigsby saw Judy notice him, standing there. She gave him a long, sidelong, sullen stare until suddenly, with a symbolism so blunt, a clue so meaningful that he felt his heart turn completely over, she yanked her hand out of Jack's. He did not seem to mind. He brought two beers from the bar. Judy stood half facing Rex, thirty feet from him. She held her glass in both hands like a child as she drank, and all the time she drank she kept staring at him, full of her unspoken, insolent questioning.

He knew then how his night would end.

ELEVEN

Happy Birthday to You

THE SUN WENT DOWN. The western sky flamed into rose and faded to bloody gray as the first stars came out. Billy Looby, lopsided and jangling with coins, worn out with the endless trundling of ice to the boats, hoarse from explaining his gallery to the incredulous, turned on the switches that made it a different party.

Up until that moment there had been an outdoor picnic flavor about it. There had been few incidents, none of them serious. No one had been thrown out as yet. There had been the incident of Jannifer Jean's exposure, which might have become more drastic had Captain Jimmy detected the man who had conducted the experiment in the process of yanking the knot loose. A young lawyer from Clewiston had found himself unable to resist the impulse to place his hand on the satiny concavity of the waist of a young woman in sun halter and shorts, a young woman he had never seen before. Unfortunately for the lawyer, she was the brand new twenty-year-old wife of a career Marine who had recently retired at thirty-seven and was taking a night off from tending bar. The lawyer never saw the blow that clicked his teeth, lifted him high onto his tiptoes, and dropped him peaceably onto his face in the dust beside the buffet. A man who liked to keep things neat rolled the lawyer under the buffet table and made himself another ham and cheese sandwich.

One of the limber dollies off the Texas yacht, *Do Tell*, heard sounds that enchanted her and, by following them to their source, was able to join a small group of devotees who, in the fading light, were bouncing green cubes off

125

the side wall of the office. She lost the forty dollars she customarily wore tucked into her bra, went twice to the yacht and borrowed a hundred, only to lose it each time.

She waited patiently for her turn at the dice and then, with the avid glitter of the compulsive gambler, announced that she was wagering herself. It took them some time to understand what she meant. As she would not let several of them cover the bet, claiming it was not only ladylike but illogical, it turned, for a time, into an auction. When she rolled, she rolled against a hundred and fifty dollars wagered by the manager of a local supermarket who could not really decide whether he'd made a good bet. She rolled eleven, verbally withdrew her original stake, and let the one fifty ride. The supermarket man covered and she threw a seven. She let the three hundred ride. He could only take forty of it.

Others came in. She threw a three-one and followed it immediately with a deuce-deuce, which was greeted by groans. She left the six hundred in. It was all covered. But after her next eleven, there wasn't enough money left in the group to cover twelve hundred. She griped about having to drag out over four hundred. It took her longer, rolling, in order, eight, four, six, nine, ten, three, five, ten, ten, six, eight, thus ending the game.

With the unthinking generosity that only a citizen of that most hospitable of all states can comprehend, and, believing that he had brought her luck, she smuggled the disconsolate supermarket man aboard the *Do Tell* and, with a jubilant heartiness, a joyous deftness, made him the happiest of men, treating him with more consideration and versatility than he would have received had he, in fact, won.

Also, before the lights went on, George Haley, using Darlene Marie Moyd to the same effect that a magician uses his scantily clad assistant to divert the eye of the curious, sold a seven thousand dollar building lot in Delightful Heights to a large bemused druggist from Kilo, Kansas, who had the quaint idea that Darlene Marie went with the deed. They whipped him in jolly fashion down to the office, opened up, prepared a deed and took his down payment. Darlene Marie had become a notary the week before.

Back at the party, just as the lights came on, the large

druggist made a minor and quite furtive attempt to verify his claim. Smiling dazzlingly, mistily, incomparably up at him, Darlene Marie swung her dainty shoe against his shin. It would have easily been a field goal from the forty-yard line. When he wiped away the tears that blurred his vision, Darlene Marie was gone. But he had a lot in a new subdivision and a pronounced limp.

The floods and spots turned the docks and much of the shore line to blinding white. But there were areas of shadow. There were lights on the boats, in the beer tent, on the buffet. Bugs swarmed eagerly to bunt their brains out on the hot lenses. The party tempo increased. Over on the beach the penny candy neon flared bravely. On Sid's hi-fi at maximum volume, Dinah Washington brayed "Love For Sale," slurring it and belting it. Lew Burgoyne and his volunteer patrol began to be more heads-up about looking for trouble.

The first casualty was a woman who stuck a high heel down between the dock boards and managed, somehow, to sit heavily on her own beer glass, sustaining lacerations more dramatic than dangerous. The second casualty was a young hotel bellhop who, confident with much beer, made his first attempt to pick a pocket, a Texan's pocket, and sustained two broken fingers, the two he had inserted in the hip pocket. The more normal mishaps were not counted—such as the eight or nine, two of them female, who passed out early—or the three, including the Clewiston lawyer, whose social mistakes had been corrected with sudden violence.

Joe Rykler had taken a short nap on the cockpit floor of the *Ampersand* and awakened much refreshed. Christy and Leo sat in the fighting chairs aboard the *Ruthless* and talked of many things. Amy Penworthy was trotting around worrying if the talent show was going to be put on too late or too early. Helen Hass, running around with a flashlight to shine on the backs of hands, had stuck sixteen hundred and forty dollars into the safe. Bud and Ginny Linder sat up in the bow of their schooner, holding hands and watching the party from the shadows as though all the people were on a big stage.

Anne Browder lay in darkness in her bed aboard the *Alrightee,* slowly consuming the biggest deadliest drink she had ever dared make herself. Tears stood in her eyes. The base of the glass was cold on her bare tummy. Joe had come aboard and knocked and hollered twice, waited and gone away. Alice Stebbins talked to old friends, and grinned and drank much beer, and felt sick and dead inside. Gus Andorian, encouraged by a shy sweet smile, pinched a plump matron with such enthusiasm that she went up into the air and landed cantering, her eyes bulging. When he came stalking after her, beaming, she showed surprising acceleration. He scowled and growled and trudged back to the *Queen Bee* for another drink.

At eight o'clock the music stopped abruptly. A lean, grinning, weasel-faced man in a grotesquely padded sports jacket stepped to the mike on the flush rear deck of the *Pieces of Seven,* whuffed into it, and then, in a piercing, carefree snarl, and with a lot of business with the eyebrows, and in the unmistakable accent of the Jersey nitespot circuit, he yelled, "Ladees an genemen! Your attenchin. Your attenchin, please! The big show is about to begin. Gather round, kiddies. Gather round." They came hurrying around from charterboat row. They packed D Dock and C Dock and the shoreline. Buffet and beer business eased slightly.

The smirking weasel introduced himself as Lonnie Guy, "fresh from the real live spots of the ennatainmint worl, inclusive of televishin. As Milty was telling me the other night, Lonnie, he said, Lonnie I love ya material. I love it so much, I use it alla time."

He paused for a laugh, heard a muted snicker, shrugged and went on. He welcomed the guests. Somehow it made it sound as if Sid Stark was putting on the party. He said, "Now we'll get this rocket off the pad with some a my own stuff."

He did an imitation of Mort Sahl, newspaper in hand. He did an adequate imitation of the Voice, gestures and delivery. But two things were wrong. He wasn't funny, and perhaps ten people in the whole group knew who the hell Mort Sahl was.

He then signaled one of Sid's people to put on a record, and he did a pantomime, fitting his gestures to the voice of Doris Day. It went over like concrete.

He did a fairy routine, and it fell flat.

"Can this maybe be Philadelphyuh? So laugh tomorrow."

In desperation, he told a joke so blue that six customers left immediately. The throng began a cadence clap. He couldn't make himself heard over it. He shrugged, sneered, and walked off. George Haley appeared squinting and blinking and grinning in the floodlights, leading Darlene Marie Moyd by the hand. She wore a white sheath top, a flaring pink skirt, gold slippers, as gleaming as her hair. She was gloriously beautiful, demure, yet confident. They got the roar of applause the weasel had been seeking.

"On this happy occasion of the birthday of somebody we all know and love, I want to present to you, my secretary, Miss Darlene Marie Moyd, the most beautiful little ole gal I've ever laid these tired ole eyes on. You all can see her any working day at my office on Broward Boulevard, Deal Daily with Haley. Darlene Marie has won herself not one, not six, but fourteen beauty contests. Lordie, I can't remember all of them, tell the truth. But tonight she's going to display the talent she showed the judges."

"Take it off!"

"Now that ain't the right attitude, Cal Steckle. I recognized your voice, and you keep quiet from here on. Darlene Marie is going to give a dramatic reading, like she did in all those contests."

There was resounding applause as he stepped back and Darlene stepped up to the microphone and composed herself.

Leo and Christy were on the edge of the crowd, out near the end of D Dock.

Darlene gave a gentle smile, cleared her throat, tilted her chin up and began to declaim:

"Ef yew can keep yo haid when all about yew air a-losin' they-yurs an a-blaimin' it on yew?"

Her voice came droning directly from the bridge of that perfect nose. It was one of those horrible, flat-land, piney-woods voices that can make three syllables grow where there was only one in the beginning.

"Good God!" Leo whispered. "Is she serious?"

"Deathly," Christy said. "She's gorgeous. If she could even twirl a baton, she'd have made Miss America—or at least Miss Florida. She makes most women look like

129

Moonbeam. But that—excuse the expression—talent! Wow!"

"I have the opinion," Leo muttered, "that her best talent couldn't be displayed to a panel of judges."

"You have a gloriously dirty mind, darling."

It was a curious agony to watch Darlene Marie. She declaimed with gestures. Sweeping, dramatic gestures which threatened to lift her up out of the last strategic half inch of the sheath top. Her large audience maintained a rapt, respectful silence.

As she neared her closing line, the weasel made another and more serious mistake in his evaluation of his audience. He came slinking up behind her with exaggerated stealth, carrying a slender stick. He ignored the low growl of protest and warning.

She swept both arms high and went onto her tippy toes for her final line. Just as she had almost completed it, he touched the stick to the tenderest curve in the rear of the pink skirt. It was one of those electric wands, highly favored by street corner Legionnaires on convention.

"Yew'll be a may-yun, my YOW!" she cried, and achieved an impressive elevation above the improvised stage, and landed whirling, spitting, slashing and weeping. Lonnie darted back out of sight. She faced her audience with a gesture of helplessness, and the great raw sound of applause squared her shoulders, dried her tears and restored her radiance.

"My goodness," Lew said to Orbie.

"You know," Orbie said, "when this here show is over, I wouldn't be surprised the boys go grab that fella and take him over in the dark past the charter boats and purely beat the livin' hell out of him."

"Caint let a terible thing like that happen," Lew said.

"No sir. We'll have to bust that up."

"Right."

"We'll go right on over there and protect that fella."

"Might get a little thirsty on the way over," Lew said.

Orbie nodded. "We can always stop and have a brew."

"Sure thing. Give us a chance to talk over just how we'll get him away from those boys that'll be beating on him by then."

"Doesn't do to rush into things. Hey, where's Leo?"

"Way up there with Christy."

"Better get my guitar. You keep an eye on him while we're on."

"How many times you told me that?"

Darlene Marie was followed by a quartet of local fishermen whose diligent practice was somewhat nullified by the sodden condition of their tenor, but their selections were loudly appreciated. George Haley had somehow taken over the M.C. chore. Next came a violent acrobatic tap dance performed by a local tavern waitress in a red leotard while her brother played a strenuous accordion. Next came a strong-man act, then a solo accordion.

Christy swallowed and said to Leo, "I'm all right?"

"You're lovely."

"Oh, sure." She had decided to go all out and had put on a silver-blue evening dress. "See you, honey." She began to make her way through the close-packed crowd on D Dock. He followed, so as to watch her from a better vantage point.

When the accordion was finished, Billy Looby fussed importantly with the lights until he'd cut them to one spot. George Haley introduced her, saying, "And this year Christy tells me she's going to be real dignified. I don't have to ask you to give her a hand."

She walked to the mike. Orbie, carrying a chair and his guitar, set himself up behind her and struck a few experimental chords. She began to sing "My Man." Her voice was a husky croak. But it was true, and her timing was almost professional.

She cast such a special, intimate spell over Leo that it was some time before he realized the crowd didn't share his pleasure. They were restless. Applause was more polite than enthusiastic when she finished.

"Thank you. And now I'm going to sing "Body and Soul.""

Before she could start, somebody started a cadence clap. Leo wanted to worm through the crowd and bash him. But others picked it up.

Christy held her hands up and said, "What's the matter?"

At least a dozen people yelled different requests simultaneously. Christy scowled at the crowd. "Don't you lint-

131

head folk dig culture?"

They yelled at her again.

"All right, all right! I'll do just one of those ranchy things one time. Sorry, Leo darling. They're twisting my arm. No, that's not the title, but we could get a song out of it." She turned and said, "Orbie, you remember that thing we worked up for this festival of dampness last year. I've still got all the words." Orbie hit some chords. "That's it. You have it, Mr. Derr." She turned back to the mike. "The song I am about to sing is entitled, 'I Was Just a Poor Fisherman's Daughter, But the Boys All Thought I was Bait.' It's a sort of a narrative type thing. Kinda tragic in a way."

She began the song. The lyrics were bawdy, without being blue. She seemed to come alive, using her face, hands and body in an enormously expressive way. Sometimes she had to stop completely for long seconds, staring solemnly out at them until they quieted down.

During one such pause, after a stanza relating her doleful experiences aboard a shrimp boat off Key West, Leo heard a familiar voice close behind him saying, ". . . no, she works in an office. Actually, a rather crude type. Hardly a lady, as I guess you can tell."

Leo whirled. Rigsby was talking to one of the Texans. Leo moved closer to him and said, "You're a son of a bitch."

"Aren't you getting terribly protective, old boy? I don't think the lassie is in need of a white knight."

"I want to talk to you. Come on."

"Right now?"

"Right now. Come on, or I'll drag you."

"Rather doubt you could, Rice. I'll come along."

They made their way through the crowd. Leo walked past the tent and up into the darkness beyond Billy's shed, Rigsby following him. He turned. "My name isn't Rice," he said, an audible tremble in his voice.

"What astounding news!"

"It's Harrison, you son of a bitch."

"That little term of endearment is getting monotonous. Is Harrison supposed to mean something to me?"

"Lucille's husband. Maybe you can remember Lucille."

There was a silence of several seconds. Leo could hear Christy's voice and the prolonged roars of laughter. The lights of cars passing on Broward touched Rigsby's face intermittently.

"Oh," Rigsby said.

"I got a complete report on you. I made my own investigation. I didn't come here by accident."

"I see." He moved back slightly. "What's on your mind?"

"I'm going to kill you."

"That's a very dull program, old boy."

"I don't think so. I'm going to enjoy it."

"The lady wasn't worth it, actually. I didn't debauch her. She wasn't good material for this cheap melodrama. We exchanged secrets, Mr. Harrison. It wasn't exactly her . . . first indiscretion."

"That's a lie."

"Oh, come now! Take out your silly gun or your silly knife so I can take it away from you."

"I'm going to kill you with my hands."

Suddenly the country gentleman accent was entirely gone.

"You what? For Chrissake, you had me standing here sweating. I was just about to suckerpunch you. With your hands! You silly bastard, you couldn't do it if you were triplets."

Leo swung as hard as he could at the man's face, so hard that he almost fell down when Rigsby sidestepped it. He moved toward the man again.

"Not now, you clown. If a beating is what you want, I'll give you one tomorrow. Not tonight. You might get lucky and bust me one time in the mouth while I'm taking you apart."

"Now!" Leo said, trying to get into position to swing again.

Lew Burgoyne suddenly appeared between them. "Hey! Hold it! How'd you sneak off without me knowing it?"

"He wants a fight. You fight him, Lew. I got better things to do."

Leo tried to get around Lew, but hard hands snapped down onto his wrists and he could not wrestle free. "We've got a date tomorrow, little man," Rigsby said. "Make it for about one. I plan to sleep late." He walked off toward the dock.

Leo struggled for a few more moments and then relaxed.

133

"You through? I can let go?"

"I'm through." Lew released him. Leo turned away, thankful for the darkness that concealed the tears on his face.

"You don't want to fight that boy," Lew said in a gentle chiding voice.

"Yes. I'm going to."

"Listen, I've seen him fight. Hell, I've fought him. Fella lives like he does, he just about has to learn to fight real good or people'd be stomping him raggedy ever' few days. I licked him, but it was hardly worth the fun at all. He's got a jaw on him like a rock, and he tucks it behind the meat on that big shoulder, and he like to hook your guts out. Minute your hands come down, pow, you get a straight right in the mouth. I tell you, the middle of me was still sore long after my face shrunk back to size. And I got a belly tough as cypress. You spent half your life sitting down in an office. Man, you don't have a chance."

"I can't help that."

"You're sure stubborn. He could actual kill you. Can't I scare you off?"

"I'm scared, Lew. But that doesn't matter."

"And when you're down, you'll get up again."

"If it takes an hour or a week or a month, I'll get up again. Somehow. You don't understand. I have to do it. There's a good reason."

Lew sighed. He pulled an unlabeled pint bottle out of his hip pocket and held it up to the faint light. "Might as well smooth off our nerves some. This here is swamp shine. They age it ten minutes afore they scoop the snakes outen it. Go first. Better get your back against the shed wall afore you tilt it."

Leo drank, gagged, choked and coughed.

"Nasty, isn't it?" Lew said, taking the bottle. "Runs maybe one-fifty proof. Listen to ole Christy go. They won't let her quit."

When Lew handed the bottle back, Leo drank again and passed the bottle. "I better let her clown all she wants to. I guess it's natural with her. I better not try any more, thanks."

"What's left isn't worth wearing out my pocket with. Come on."

They split it. Lew tossed the bottle into the darkness. A woman yelped and a man yelled, "Watch it, you clumsy jerk!"

"Sorry, old buddy," Lew said, and they walked down toward the lights and the sound of Christy's voice.

A few moments after they got there, the crowd finally let Christy go. She and Leo found each other in the crush and went aboard the *Shifless*.

As soon as the door was shut, she said, "Darling, they *made* me do the stuff they wanted to hear."

"Sperfectly all right," he said solemnly. "Wunnerful."

She peered at him. "Is that a glaze I see?"

"I love you truly."

"Wow!"

"Some stuff Lew had. Battery acid, possibly."

"Shine!" She sighed. "Wouldn't it be easier to just get somebody to club you on the head?"

"I tried that first."

"Turn your back while I go informal."

"Happy to help."

"None of that, lad. I want to hear Alice's speech. And those imitation Maguire sisters are the last act, and she's usually great."

After Orbie had put his guitar away, he located Lew. "Like to wore my fingers down to nothing. Give me a whack on that shine."

"I used it up," Lew said, and as Orbie stared at him indignantly, he went on to explain where and how.

"So they'll just fight then, tomorrow," Orbie said. "Christy'll be glad to know that's all that's going to happen."

"I don't know it's anything to be so glad about, damn it."

"What do you mean?"

"He won't quit."

"A man has to take a licking sometimes."

"After the time they sunk the can I was on in the Slot, and the Marines got to use us on account of they were short and things were busy on the island, I got into one of those Banzai parties at first light. Had me a carbine. I didn't know Japs grew as big as the Jap major who came a-running toward my hole, yelling and waving a big damn sword. It went on like slow motion. I put six holes in him, and he

135

acted like I was throwing rice at him. He was stone dead, but he was still on his feet and he was running, because he hadn't got the message. He didn't fall dead until he'd put such a hell of a crease in my helmet with that sword, it knocked me cold as a bat's ass, and then he fell dead into my hole right on top of me."

"I get your message."

"Rigsby'll tear everything loose in the middle of that man, and he'll get up for more. Except for Christy, I'd say it's none of my business. Or yours."

"What you figure on doing?"

"I wisht there was some damn way of slowing Rigsby down some before the fight, sort of give Leo more chance."

"You want to beat on him a little?"

"Not me. I had that one time. Turned me into an old, old man. How about you?"

"Hell, I can't even lick him, Lew."

"Couldn't you wear him down like he's licking you?"

"Seems to me like there's something wrong with that idea someplace."

"Maybe we can think of something before noon tomorrow."

"Hey, there's Alice." They moved closer.

Billy had put all the lights back on. Big Alice stepped to the mike with her curious lightness and grace and grinned out at them.

"Somebody has been rumoring it around, folks, that this isn't going to get into the society news. Anyhow, it's nice to be thirty-nine again. You all don't give a damn about my birthday. It's just a big fat excuse to get drunk and noisy. You're noisy all right. You're disturbing the rich people way the hell and gone over in Cat Cay. The beer drunk already tonight would float any boat in this basin, except maybe that mangy scow from Texas. That boat is so full of money it's heavy.

"Quiet down now. I want to be serious. Drink up, live it up, because this is the last one. Not my last birthday, please God, but the last surprise birthday party at the Stebbins' Marina. I'm selling." She looked over into the darkness. "You can start fixing the papers up any time, George."

"They're all ready."

136

"God knows I don't want to sell. Don't know why I'm so reluctant to get shut of this crummy, rickety, half-ass old boatyard. I'd rather lose an arm. After taxes, insurance and expenses, I just about make eating money, and that's the truth. They've been telling me I don't charge you people enough, but God knows I don't furnish much to charge you for. Seems I got to be forced out of here because this is turning into too important a part of town, and I'm operating an eyesore. It's either sell, or get closed down for something they can think up easy enough. Maybe for having parties like this. I'm getting a good enough price, I guess. But nobody gets much joy out of somebody twisting their arm.

"So this part of my life is over. Don't know where the hell I'll go or what I'll do. They'll push all you people out and tear everything down and build it up again pretty. And expensive. I'm sorry about that. Can't help it. I'm sorriest about those who've made this their home for years. The best friends I've ever had."

Her voice had thickened, and a new wetness under her eyes glinted in the brightness of the lights.

"So this is the last party, folks. And . . . thanks."

George moved to the mike and began to boom, "Happy Birthday to you . . ." The crowd picked it up, sang it more slowly than the tempo with which George had started it. Alice stood until it was over and then quietly walked away.

"Just a moment!" George brayed. "Just a little word of explanation. This city is growing fast. We need a first-class marina. A bunch of public spirited men are buying it at a fair price and they're going to make it one of the showplaces of . . ."

Some woman with diesel-horn lungs yelled a word so shockingly loud and shockingly crude that it stopped George dead and moved him half a step back from the mike. When he tried to continue, dozens of people were yelling at him. He gave up.

"God damn," Lew said to Orbie.

"Never thought she would."

"She's got to. You heard her."

"I just plain hate to see it happen, Lew. Everything keeps changing, and nothing ever changes for the better."

137

"I tell you one thing. It's going to cost one hell of a lot more to live on a boat around here. Everybody will scatter and they'll never get back together again, all in the same place."

"It's just not fair!" Christy said intensely to Leo. "It's not fair!"

"Progress."

"Darling, you look like a broiled owl."

He bowed. "Thank you."

"Poor Alice."

"Make faces, honey. Make me laugh. I feel down."

"Like this?"

"Yes. Hold it."

"Huh? Hey, how could you kiss a face like that?"

"It was easy. Try another."

"I've got about fifteen good ones."

"Run through 'em twice. Tireless Leo. I'm fueled up with shine."

"Then let's take tireless Leo off to a privater place, maybe."

"Snexcellent suggesh—suggestion. Hearten me for the morrow, love."

"What happens tomorrow?"

"Nothing of any importance."

"Except your important hangover."

TWELVE

Happy Something

THE TALENT SHOW WAS, in one sense, the peak of the evening. After it ended at nine fifteen, the party began to suffer a certain amount of attrition. But the ones who departed were the more sedate guests, and those who felt they had been grossly insulted in one way or another, and those who were in haste to consummate new friendships, as well as the few who had sustained injuries, or fallen off docks and boats, or had a meager tolerance for alcohol.

A party is a capsule lesson in the theories of Darwin. Those unsuited to the environment drop off first. What is left is the hard core, the tireless ones of vim and appetite who, given more elbow room, can duplicate the noise and confusion of a larger group. And they are no longer subject to the repressive effects of the potential disapproval of the sedate ones.

At quarter to ten, Lew Burgoyne heard a concerted rhythmic roaring, like organized cheering, coming from the direction of charterboat row. He hurried in that direction. People were in a big circle around one of the dim dock lights.

"It's just old Captain Jimmy thinkin' he's a goat agin," Dave Harran said to Lew as he joined the group. "They're eggin' him on something terrible."

Lew saw Jannifer Jean in the group, her usually placid face expressing avidity and a certain contempt. Captain Jimmy was on his hands and knees about eight feet from the slender iron light pole. He was hatless. Weather had turned the lower half of his face to leather. His forehead, always protected from the sun, was high, white and somehow pathetic. There were several red lumps on it, one of them bleeding.

"Go!" they yelled in unison. "Go! Go!"

Captain Jimmy trundled forward, picking up speed, and banged his head with such force against the lamp standard that the high light swayed back and forth, and the rebound knocked him back onto his haunches. He backed away from it as the spectators sighed, shook his head and made a whinnying noise. Lew knew there was no point in trying to stop him. It could even be dangerous. After he had decided he was a goat, he'd bite you if you gave him a chance.

"Go, go, go!"

He moved again, slammed into the pole, and rolled quietly onto his back, out cold. That was the way it always ended. The crowd dispersed. Lew and Dave went and picked him up easily.

"Wheah yuh goan?" Moonbeam demanded.

"Up to the trailer."

"Putum ona boat, huh."

"Better put him to bed in the trailer."

"Putumonagahdamnboat!" she shrieked.

"Okay, okay, okay." They took Captain Jimmy aboard his *Jimmy-Jan* and loaded him into a bunk.

Lew wondered about her insistence. He found out, by accident, an hour later, when he remembered a forgotten bottle of shine in the glove compartment of his old car and took a shortcut toward the parking lot. Captain Jimmy's trailer was a home-made job on responsive rickety springs. It was in darkness. Lew, hearing the rock and clitter of the springs, stopped and stared at it until his eyes became used to the darkness and he could see the visible bounding of the boxlike structure and the half a dozen men loosely cued up by the door. The motion died away. A man came out and one went in. The motion began again. Lew estimated that the old springs would receive the equivalent of transcontinental milage before the night was over.

The man who had come out came swaggering over toward Lew. "That you, Lew?"

"Who is it?"

"Me. Pete." It was the mechanic brother of the waitress

who had done the violent tap dance.

"You don't much care what you do."

"It ain't that bad."

"What's she charging?"

"Well, it's sort of five dollars."

"What the hell you mean, sort of."

"Come over by the light." They walked over. Pete handed him a piece of white paper.

"What the hell is this?"

"You know Pig Wallace, the surveyor?"

"Sure."

"Once we found out she was hustling, we didn't have no five dollars apiece, and no friends to loan us. Pig had this kind of drawing paper in the car and some shears, and we used us the onliest one buck we had for a sample. We made a stack. Then I yanked the main electric on the trailer so she can't check. Shut your eyes and feel it. Feels like money, don't it?"

"Doesn't she wonder if she isn't getting a one instead of a five?"

"We been giving her five of them. You crumple them some first. Pig and me, we're selling five of these for a buck, and we're doing pretty good. You want five."

"I tell you, I'd have no use for them, Pete. My God, she's going to be one crazy-mad bitch come morning."

"That's too damn bad, Lew. I got to go round up some more business. Looks like maybe we're going to have to cut up some more paper, this keeps up. Pig's got a lot left, in big sheets."

Shortly before eleven o'clock, Lew and Marty Urban had an opportunity to eject a paying customer. He was a local cab driver, a large sloppy man named Shed Stauffler, and a quickly assembled kangaroo court decided that his offense merited parabolic ejection. Shed agreed, with a certain solemnity and even cooperated in an uncoordinated fashion. He was ashamed of himself. He yearned for punishment.

He had been caught red-handed lumbering off into the darkness hugging the penultimate keg of beer to his chest. His explanation that it was just a nightcap seemed feeble.

Enough cars had left the parking lot to provide a clear

space. A group of experts watched the proceedings narrowly. Lew's coordination was blurred by shine. He took the ankles and Marty took the wrists. They swung him three times and let go the fourth time. Their grunt of final effort mingled with Shed's howl of alarm. He turned in the air and landed so thunderously on the seat of his baggy pants that it bounced him neatly back onto his feet. After his moment of surprise, he turned and bowed, and then walked with a certain dignity to his cab and went to sleep in the back seat. It was agreed that they had done exceptionally well with so large a man.

It was at about this time that Alice Stebbins went to bed. Unlike other years, she had no heart for the festivities. She was tired of having people tell her, with all the ponderous emotionality of alcohol, how sorry they were. The more volatile had dampened her blouse with their tears.

The bright lights on the docks made unfamiliar patterns on the ceiling. The sounds of party came through the window screens. The music was not as loud. There were unidentifiable yelps and whinnies. One dogged group was trying to sing "Row, Row, Row Your Boat." In spite of their most determined efforts to sing it as a round, they kept getting mixed up and finishing all together. Then there would be a loud, angry, vicious argument about whose fault it was before they started again.

A stranger, walking by below her window said, ". . . so she says you don't like the way I gaffed your damn fish and I said no the way you did it I could have lost it and she said if that's the way you want to be about it I quit and before I could grab her she throws overboard the gaff, the fish, the rod and reel, the mop, the boat hook and the Goddamn lunch and then she says take me home, for Chrissake, and starts crying . . ."

Suddenly she heard the familiar, ponderous creaking of the stairs, like a trained bear climbing a stepladder, and she smiled in the darkness. Gus fumbled his way into the apartment, and in a whisper like cracking a steam valve, said, "Alice! You here?

"Was unlock down there," he whispered. "Not safe for you. Any dronk bum could come in, yes?"

In a little while he came into the bed beside her. It

142

dipped under his weight. He sighed heavily. When she was in his arms it took her a few moments to identify the odd little sounds he was making. She touched his eyelids with her fingertips and said, "Why, you're crying, you big boobie. Now . . . now you've got me doing it too."

He held her, snuffled against her throat, "So damn lonesome all of a sudden," he mumbled. "Is no good at all."

At midnight, due to a serious underestimation of the amount of beer required, the tent bar was forced to close. Every scrap of food was gone. Those who had left bottles with the bartenders reclaimed them, some quarreling bitterly about the meager amount left. The rule about carrying bottles around on the person was relaxed to compensate for the new conditions.

Also at midnight, as Orbie was standing near the *Lullaby* talking to Sim and Gloria Gallowell, they heard a thin and frantic male voice yelling, "Help! Help!" It came from over by charterboat row. The yells were smothered by distant sounds of conflict.

Orbie said, "You know, that could be that fella that give Darlene Marie the boost with that buzz stick."

"Could be at that," Sim said. "Made himself unpopular with the boys, doing a thing like that. Funny they took so long to get him."

"I heard a while back they were having a time getting him off Sid's boat."

"You'd better *do* something!" Gloria said. "He isn't real strong looking. They could kill him over there."

"I guess we're just about to," Sim said. "Aren't we just about to, Orbie?"

"Let's just amble on over there."

"Don't you start to fighting, honey," Gloria said. "You just wait right here where it's nice and light. We'll take care of this and then we'll all go on home. Where's Marty and Mary Lee."

"I guess they're still on that Texas boat, honey. That party is getting bigger and bigger. Hurry before they kill that poor man. Please hurry!"

Orbie and Sim headed toward the disturbance, walking without particular haste. When they were fifty feet away, somebody grabbed Orbie's arm from behind and

143

whirled him so violently that Orbie came dangerously close to belting Jack Engly in the face.

"Where's Judy?" Jack demanded. "You seen Judy?"

"No, I haven't seen her for a long time."

"Me either," Sim said.

"I kinda dozed off sitting aboard my boat and she was there and then she wasn't. You see her, you tell her I'm looking for her."

The sound of battle had stopped. Sim and Orbie joined the group of half a dozen protectors of Southern womanhood. They were standing looking down at Lonnie Guy, one of them squatting beside him, holding a match. Lonnie was a mess. An argument was going on. Two men felt they hadn't been given a chance at him. The others, honor satisfied, were worried about overdoing it.

"All right, all right," Sim said. "Somebody go draw a bucket. Is he breathing, Mike?"

"A little bit, now and again, Sim."

After the second slosh with a bucket of salt water, Lonnie groaned and rolled over. Sim and Orbie picked him up, each holding him by an arm, and walked him back toward the *Pieces of Seven,* followed for half the distance by two men pleading for just one little chop more. Lonnie's chin bobbed on his chest. His nose lay neatly against his right cheek. His legs flapped loosely in his attempt to walk, and he dribbled a few tooth fragments.

"Sure messed him," Sim said.

"Be a good idea to get a doctor. They can call. Sid's got a phone strung onto that Chris of his."

Gloria was where they had left her. She had been joined by Leo and Christy. Lonnie was walking a little better, but he didn't look any better. "We'll unload him and be right back, kids," Orbie said.

They used the little portable ladderway on the port side of the *Pieces of Seven* to walk him aboard. Francesca Portoni came charging up to them, black hair whipping, black eyes flashing, cinematic bosom heaving. "What ees thees!"

"It's a prominent figger in the entertainment world," Orbie said. "Where's Sid?"

She made a sweeping gesture that nearly tipped her off her bare feet. "Pass out. Everybody ees pass out, total. I

144

am so bore. Ees a big mess all over." She paused and looked more closely at Lonnie Guy. *"Sangre de la Madonna!"* she said in an awed tone.

She told them where to put him. She was phoning a doctor when they left.

Joe Rykler had heard the sounds of combat, and though they were nearby, they seemed vastly unimportant to him. He was more concerned with listening to himself and trying to figure out what he was saying. He was on his back on something that had a rubbery softness. He was looking up at the stars. There was a woman in the curve of his right arm. Just beyond her, a sonorous, carefully articulated male voice said, "Nebraska, Nevada, New Hampshire."

Joe stopped listening to his own sad fuzzy voice and hiked himself up just long enough to orient himself before the woman yanked him back down. He was over in charterboat row, on some kind of big bulbous rubberized air mattress on the bow deck of the *Fleetermouse.*

"Whassamarra, honey?" the woman said.

"Who are you?"

"There you go again," she said petulantly. "Can't you keep track. Alla time you gotta be clued. You muss be drunk. I'm Beezie, baby. Ole Beezie Hooper."

"Oh."

"New Jersey, New Mexico, New York," the man just beyond her said. She lay between them.

"Who's *that?*"

"I tole you ninety times, Joey. Sa house guest me and Stan. Peter. He says the states to make sure he's not stinking. Then the pres'dents, and finally the atomic table, but he never gets all the way through. Talk sad some more. I wanna cry some more." She rolled against him and began to chomp at the lower half of his face like a person trying to eat an apple. Joe found it unpleasant.

"North Carolina, North Dakota, Ohio," the man said.

Joe pushed her away and said, "Where's Stan?"

"Piffle on him. Sour, dirry ole louse. It's you and me against all of 'um. Make me cry."

"Oklahoma, Oregon, Pennsylvania." He could hear a dull mumbling of voices from the cockpit of the boat, identified it as a semi-comprehensible political argument.

Then a voice was calling. "Joe! Joe Rykler!" He sensed urgency in the voice. He recognized Amy Penworthy's voice. He sat up. Beezie yanked him down so hard he bounced. He pushed her away and scrambled up, lost his footing and nearly pitched overboard.

"Come back here, you moron!" Beezie yelled.

He went gingerly down the side deck, stepped over onto the narrow access dock and walked ashore. His legs felt unreliable.

"Amy?"

She came up to him and said in a low voice, "I've been looking all over. Are you drunk?"

"You've been looking for me to ask me that?"

"You don't seem too bad, I guess. It's Anne."

Something went on in his head, like rolling up a gauze screen that separated the audience from the action on the stage.

"What about Anne?"

"You're hurting my arm. About half an hour ago I went aboard the *Alrightee*. She was packing a bag. She was tight and she was crying. I asked her what she was doing. She said she was going on a cruise on that Texas boat. They invited her, she said. She said she'd be gone for weeks and weeks. I couldn't do anything with her. I asked her why she was doing such a crazy thing and she said so you could stop being in love with her, and she said she wasn't any damn good and it was time to prove it. I don't know what to do, and I thought . . ."

Then he was taking long strides, and Amy was trotting along behind him. He was consciously taking deep breaths in an effort to clear his head completely.

Suddenly a tall figure blocked his path. "You seen Judy?" Jack Engly demanded.

"Get out of the way!"

"I want to know, you seen Judy."

"No. No, I haven't seen Judy."

He walked on. Behind him he heard Jack asking Amy. He walked by a group near the *Lullaby*—Leo, Christy, Orbie, Sim, Gloria. They spoke but he did not answer.

One long narrow gangplank stretched from the T of D Dock to the forward weather deck of the *Do Tell*. It was unguarded. Calypso was coming over the yacht's speaker system. A sweaty clot of enthusiasts were accompanying it with improvised percussion instruments, clanging and banging while couples danced with more abandon than taste on the shadowy decks.

He prowled the decks and did not find Anne. He went below. There was an incongruous game of dominos in the main lounge, and one man in pajamas calmly reading a paper with a steaming mug of coffee beside him. A huge brown man was trundling around and around on his hands and knees, giving, from time to time, a realistic whinny. A dainty little blonde rode on his back, a look of happy ecstasy on her face, saying, "Gidyap, gidyap, horsie-horsie."

Joe paused to let them go by and went to the man reading the paper. "I'm looking for Miss Browder."

He put the paper down and frowned. "Who?"

"Miss Browder. A tall blonde girl. Her name is Anne. Somebody invited her to come on your cruise with you."

"Whoa!" the man roared. The circling horse came to a stop and lifted its head inquiringly. "Bunny, you know about anybody inviting some gal along?"

"That was B. J. He asked me if it was okay. We got room so I said sure. Gidyap, horsie-horsie."

"Hold on. This fella is looking for the gal."

"She went off to pack. Should be back aboard now."

"I told you and I told B. J. and I told everybody else, no bringing no more women aboard on this here cruise unless I say okay. It turns out to be somebody's wife, and we got us all kind of fuss, like over in Clearwater. You buck that little gal off, horsie, and he'p this man find his girl."

Bunny rose to an impressive muscular height and the little blonde slid off, pouting. "C'mawn," Bunny said to Joe. They went forward, along a narrow corridor with stateroom doors on either side, a deep soft carpet on the deck, soft bulkhead lights at spaced intervals.

"There's ole B. J.," Bunny said.

A big florid man with hair and brows baked to sand white was thumping a stateroom door and pleading with someone inside.

As they came up to him, Bunny said, "What's goin' on, boy?"

"She's done locked me out. Ain't that a hell of a thing?

Carrying on something fierce. Crying and all. Figure I could just get aholt of her one time I could gentle her down."

"This that Anne girl?"

"Sure is."

"Old Jimbo is going to chew you good, boy."

"What for? She went and packed her stuff. I'm not kidnaping her."

Anne's voice was suddenly clear, calling out just on the other side of the locked door, distorted with fright and despair. "Help me! He won't let me get off the boat! He won't let me go! I changed my mind. Please help me, whoever's out there. Get the police."

Bunny said, "Oh, no, you're not kidnaping her. Not a little bit. She's happy as can be."

"Coulda handled it polite and easy," B. J. said sullenly.

"It's me," Joe called. "Joe."

"Help me, Joe!"

"It's okay to unlock and come out," Bunny yelled. "This fella will take you ashore, gal."

"Joe?"

"It's all right, honey."

The lock clicked. The door opened cautiously. The soft light shone on her tear-stained face, her apprehensive eyes. Joe took her suitcase and walked her along the corridor, his hand on her waist. She walked with shoulders hunched, head down.

Bunny said, "Sorry about this thing, mister. B. J. he gets himself worked up sometimes."

It is peculiar that any act of special violence seems to have a timing that suits the time and the place, as though on some subliminal level, it draws its own unsuspecting audience, sets its own horrible stage.

The stage was set for the violence that ended the birthday party in the following manner. Leo and Christy, discovering a mutual ravenous hunger, started toward the parking lot with the intention of driving to an all-night restaurant. On the way to the parking lot they met Lew Burgoyne. In the distance the three of them could hear Jack Engly calling his wife.

Lew said, "He's sure anxious to find that little girl."

148

"If he does, he'll wish he hadn't," Christy said.

"I've been thinking that too," Leo said. "About half an hour ago Christy looked out the cabin port of my boat and saw Rigsby sneaking her onto the *Angel*."

"The hell you say!"

"That's right," Christy said.

"Should have guessed it," Lew muttered. They went on to the parking lot and found Christy's car hopelessly blocked in by two other cars, so they turned and went back toward D Dock, walking hand in hand, planning to see what they could find to eat aboard the *Shifless*.

After they had left to go to the lot, Lew had stood in the darkness and then had seen a fine solution to the problem he and Orbie had discussed. So he set off at a trot toward the sound of Jack's voice.

"Did you find her?" Jack asked anxiously.

"Not exactly, but I got me an idea."

"What?"

"Maybe if a fella should take a look aboard the *Angel* . . ."

"No!" Engly whispered. "No!"

"It's just an idea."

As Jack hurried toward D Dock, Lew followed slowly, grinning, thinking of the battering Rigsby would take. He arrived at D Dock at the same time as Leo and Christy. The group standing near the *Lullaby* was staring along the bright white length of the dock, staring at Jack Engly striding out toward the end of the dock.

Orbie turned and looked at Lew and said, "What the hell are you grinning about?"

"Told him Judy was with Rex. Jack'll soften him up some."

Orbie's face was utterly blank for a moment, then became tight with anger. "You plain damn fool! He stopped dead right here. Didn't say a word to me. Jumped onto the *Lullaby* and grabbed the short tarpon gaff off the port rack and jumped back on the dock and took off. Come on!"

He turned and started to run after Engly. After a shocked pause, the other men began to trot after him. A short tarpon gaff is a cruel hook about a foot long, fashioned of half inch steel, with about three inches between the needle point and the shank. The shank is welded to a

149

six-inch crosspiece of one-inch bar stock which forms the hand grip.

Two further coincidences heightened tension. Just as Engly reached that point of the dock directly astern of the *Angel,* Joe came off the gangplank of the *Do Tell,* his arm still around Anne. The other coincidence was wickedly effective. The stack of Calypso records on the *Do Tell* ended. And in the sudden silence came plump Judy's cat-yelps of love, her wild ululations, muffled by the closed doors of the trunk cabin.

Jack Engly stood as though he had taken a bullet in the heart. The muscles of his lean back bulged the sweat-damp T shirt, his arms hung long, raw, brown and powerful in the white glare of the temporary floodlights. His knuckles were pale where his hand gripped the gaff. He shook his head violently.

Orbie had almost reached him, yelling his name, when Engly sprang like a great cat. He pounced lightly down into the cockpit, eeled past the wheel and a stay, kicked the doors open, grabbed the top of the trunk cabin, swung his legs through, arching his back to drop out of sight into the darkness of the roomy cabin amidships. Wild things move that way, in a flickering of such speed it seems supernatural—a city cat speeding on tiptoe up the precarious slant of a mountain of trash to nail the random mouse inside a rusty bucket.

One second after they heard the thud of his feet as he landed below, the woman began to scream. It was a sound that seemed to chill the sweat of the hot night. She screamed with all her might with every breath she took. They could tell she was holding her mouth wide and flat. It was a cry of terror and disgust and madness. The human throat is not constructed to endure such a sound. In each additional scream there was an accretion of hoarseness. It was obvious that she would continue to make that sound until the voice was utterly gone and continue beyond that, the lungs exploding a rush of air through the silenced throat in idiot rhythm.

There was no music on the dock to screen the sound she was making. It was atavistic, penetrating all layers of drunkenness except with those who were unconscious. It drew the people from the mainland and the other docks and the boats, some hurrying, some approaching with evident reluctance.

Orbie started to go aboard, then made a gesture of helplessness and resignation. There were shouts of alarm and interrogation. Mingled with the woman's screams and the other sounds, there was a violent thumping sound. Jack Engly reappeared, bent forward from the waist, moving slowly, his face, in the white glare of the floods, a corroded mask of effort, lips pulled back from his teeth, blue eyes sickeningly blank. He plodded forward, pulling. Muscles ridged his right arm.

He pulled Rigsby out into the brilliance of the lights. Rigsby was on the gaff, naked. The point had entered the front of his throat and emerged from the nape of his neck, a full inch off center. Rigsby writhed and spasmed, trying to grasp the wrist of the hand that held the gaff, trying to get his legs under him. The growing crowd moved back, making an odd simultaneous sound like the sigh of a great weary animal.

Rigsby's struggles grew less violent. Jack Engly crawled up onto the dock, crouching. With a final heave, a monstrous, bone-cracking effort, he came erect, yanking the limp body up onto the dock and, with a most dextrous and professional motion, slipping the gaff out the instant the weight was off his arm. Rigsby landed heavily on his side. His head thumped the dock timbers. He rolled half onto his face. Blood spread under the throat. A brown hand crawled a little way on its fingers. It shuddered and then was suddenly flat and soft against the dock. Too flat, too soft, too significantly motionless.

The woman-screams, clotted with hoarseness, verging on madness, continued.

Engly looked once at the body, then turned slowly and began to walk toward shore, a jerky, mechanical, uncoordinated walk. They jumped aboard boats to give him all the room he might need. Lew Burgoyne blocked his way. Engly stopped and stared beyond him.

"Hand me the gaff, Jack. You're scarin' folks."

Engly handed it to him without comment. Two women had fainted. Anne Browder had broken away from Joe

151

and gone aboard the *Angel* to see what she could do for Judy Engly. Somebody mercifully threw a tarp over the body. Somebody else phoned the police. In a little while they heard the sirens in the night.

At four in the morning, after Judy had been given a shot that dropped her into unconsciousness and had been taken to the Elihu Beach Memorial Hospital, and after the body had been taken to the city morgue, and Jack Engly taken in for interrogation, after the temporary dock lights were off, the reporters and photographers gone, the last revelers silenced, Leo and Christy drove over to the beach, left the car and walked a long long way on the packed sand left by the outgoing tide, walked in what was left of the moonlight. He held her hand as they walked. They talked little. There was nothing to say.

Finally they sat in the dry sand up beyond the high tide line and waited to watch the sunrise.

"Even for a man like that, it was too . . ."

"I know, darling."

"I couldn't have killed him. I could thump my chest and make loud and dramatic noises, but now I know I couldn't have killed him."

"I knew that too."

"I couldn't kill anybody, actually. Be jury and judge and hangman. Not coldly like that. Maybe in defence of home or woman. As, in a way, Jack did. But . . ."

"I know what you are, darling. And love what you are."

"Foolish girl."

"Sure. Foolish and lucky, maybe."

There was a red line in the east, and then the long slow explosion of the dawn, and a red sun climbing out of the sea.

She leaned closer and kissed the corner of his mouth. "May I be right corny, Mister Leo?"

"You have permission."

"See? Sunrise. New beginning. Symbolic. New beginning for us, because the other is all over now. You've toyed with my affections, and you're rich and pretty, so I demand marriage."

"I was juss fixin' to ask you, Miz Yale."

152

THIRTEEN

THIS IS A LONG PASSAGE from a very long letter written several years later by Joe Rykler to an old friend and editor who stayed with Joe for the two weeks directly following the birthday party.

Dear Sam,

I can understand your feverish concern about what happened to all the people you met down here. It is because you are a very neat man, and you have to have everything tied up. It is the same reason you over-edit my copy.

Wouldn't you rather be left in the dark, and just imagine what happened to everybody? And if, as you said, it has been bothering you, why did you have to wait so long? I couldn't even remember some of this stuff and had to go ask people. And you knew all the names. What did you do? Take notes?

I will not take them in any special order. Helen Hass is now Mrs. Walter Biggerts. You didn't meet him. She met hm at an adult education course, and he was a very shiftless, helpless, poorly organized guy, and presto, she had an outlet for all those terrifying organizational energies of hers. He is now totally organized, but looks a little haunted, and the sole by-product of this union, thus far, is being raised in accord with the fattest rule books in the business.

I guess you want to know particularly about Captain Jimmy and his Jannifer Jean on account of you were so knocked out by that story of the pieces of paper the size of money. It turned out it was just too good a story, and finally poor Captain Jimmy heard it from a man in a bar who didn't know who Captain Jimmy was. Captain Jimmy asked enough questions to be absolutely sure, and then he went on a five-day drunk. After he out-sat the hangover, he got him a gaff handle and he beat Moonbeam into a cringing lump of contrition, a very long and noisy process. It took half a dozen of those sessions to give her a constructive attitude toward marriage. She's still sloppy, but she does the cooking and wears clothes that cover her, and jumps to attention when Captain Jimmy snaps his fingers. In typical Southern tradition, he is keeping her barefoot and pregnant, and she is not likely to get into any more trouble.

Dink Western had a little mishap which pleased everybody. He took a charter out a while back. Dave Harran wasn't with him. Dink managed to fall overboard. The tourists couldn't run the boat, but they sure as hell tried. They made a big circle and came back after him at full cruising speed and ran right the hell over him. Lew Burgoyne bought the *Bally-Hey* from the widow and, after extensive repairs and cleaning and repainting, turned it over to Dave to operate for him.

That drunken Beezie I introduced you to got a quick divorce over a year ago and went to live on her alimony in Cuernavaca with an old buddy of hers named Gloria Garvey.

About Rex Rigsby, they couldn't turn up any will or any heirs, so they buried him at his expense and stuck the rest of his dough in an escrow account and auctioned off the *Angel*. A thousand years from now the State of Florida will grab hold of the money. There were four mourners at the services, all female. Those Decklin brothers made a big fat public relations gesture by bidding the high bid on the *Angel* and then turning it over to the local Sea Scouts.

That sweet guy, Orbie Derr, finally got fed with those batches of Bitty-Beddy girls, so he quit and got a job as hired captain of something big and fast called the *Can-Do*. A constructon outfit owns it, and they send no women down, so Orbie's nerves are a lot better.

I guess you read about old Gus Andorian. The wire

154

services picked up the full story of that jam he got into about six months after the party. A beery episode of a truly gargantuan quaintness. So all the horrified daughters and their husbands tried to lawyer the hell out of him, getting him declared incompetent and released in their custody and so on, so they could dole his pension out to him. But Gus got hold of a smart lawyer too, and he didn't like the advice his boy gave him, but it was his best out, so after a lot of grumbling and sighing, he married Alice Stebbins, and he's been astonished ever since that she's made no cut in his beer ration.

You probably read about Sid Stark, too, Sam. I guess people got tired of trying to serve those papers on him. That's why they hired the expert to come down and blow a great big hole in his chest. An ex-wife attached the boat for back alimony, and his pals gave him one hell of a big funeral in Jersey. I heard the other day that Francesca Portoni, billed as Mary Flying Feather, the Seminole Princess, is doing a real frantic strip in a Miami Beach joint.

You had the good sense to dislike George Haley on sight, I remember, and this should make you feel cozy. Mrs. George Haley finally caught George and Darlene in bed in a demonstration house in Delightful Heights. George had an exclusive listing on the house. After the divorce Darlene's several large male relatives convinced George it would be nice if he were to remarry. The lovely Darlene has put on thirty pounds, developed a piercing whine, let her hair turn back to mouse, won't work in the office, is a slob around the house, and is so savagely jealous and possessive she makes the first Mrs. Haley seem like the most liberal of women.

Those nice kids, Bud and Ginny Linder, had twins, and then a single, and now she's in a delicate condition again. They're going to go around the world—after the children are grown.

I know you followed the accounts of Jack Engly's trial. It's a good thing Jack wouldn't say a word. Orbie and Lew got up there and testified they saw Rigsby forcing Judy aboard the *Angel*, and they testified they heard her screaming for help when Jack went aboard. Judy testified that was just the way it happened. After a lot of horse trading by the lawyers, they let it go through as a plea of guilty to manslaughter, so he ended up with time at Raiford. He ought to be out soon. The boat was leased and Judy went off to live with his people. They say that before they took him away, he and Judy made it up.

I guess it was evident to you, Sam, as it was to everybody, that Leo and Christy had a thing for each other. But you don't know how the marina thing worked out. Those Decklins tried to use the wild party and the killing as an excuse to cut their offering price way down, so Alice took the problem to Leo. He is a mild guy you would think, but by the time he got some hungry lawyers working on the whole thing, those Decklins were ready to admit they'd backed into a hot stove. Leo went in as a partner with Alice, took the marina off the market and arranged to use the money he paid Alice to improve the place.

He went North and wound up his affairs up there and brought his sons down to attend his wedding to Christy.

There have been a lot of improvements, but not too many. The flavor is the same here at D Dock. The place runs smoothly and it makes money and they stick every dime they can back into more improvements. Leo and Christy live aboard the *Shifless* and the boys live aboard the *Ruthless*. Nobody wants to move into a house yet. But Christy is bloomingly pregnant, way out here to here, and she calls herself "the right man's burden, or, exemption alley, foe of the revenuers." So maybe there'll have to be a house in their future.

Anne is right here asking me if I'm writing a book or a letter. She says it's the right time of day to go over to the beach for a swim. Sam, this is the third time for me, and the perfect time and the last time. This girl is suitable. You remember how jumpy she was when you met her. I've never told you this before, and I wouldn't tell everybody, but for once in his life, Joe Rykler made the right move.

I took her down to the Keys right after you left. I gave her more steak and bourbon and exercise than she'd ever seen before. I kept her in a state of total exhaustion and relaxation. And on the tenth evening, Sam, she

156

stopped being neurotic about a lot of things and turned into one hell of a lot of woman all of a sudden. So I brought her back and married her and she's stayed that way.

Well, enough of history, old buddy. Let's get down to the present. I've got your revision suggestions on the book, old buddy, and I think you're crazy as hell. You're a nit-picker. For example, take another look at your copy of the third chapter and tell me why I should leave out the funniest character in the book. . . .

JOHN D. MacDONALD

The Travis McGee Series

Follow the quests of Travis McGee, amiable and incurable tilter at conformity, boat-bum Quixote, hopeless sucker for starving kittens, women in distress, and large, loose sums of money.

☐ THE DEEP BLUE GOOD-BY	14176	$2.25
☐ NIGHTMARE IN PINK	14259	$2.25
☐ A PURPLE PLACE FOR DYING	14219	$2.25
☐ THE QUICK RED FOX	14264	$2.25
☐ A DEADLY SHADE OF GOLD	14221	$2.50
☐ BRIGHT ORANGE FOR THE SHROUD	14243	$2.50
☐ DARKER THAN AMBER	14162	$2.50
☐ ONE FEARFUL YELLOW EYE	14146	$2.50
☐ PALE GRAY FOR GUILT	14148	$2.50
☐ THE GIRL IN THE PLAIN BROWN WRAPPER	14256	$2.25
☐ DRESS HER IN INDIGO	14170	$2.50
☐ THE LONG LAVENDER LOOK	13834	$2.50
☐ A TAN AND SANDY SILENCE	14220	$2.50
☐ THE SCARLET RUSE	13952	$2.50
☐ THE TURQUOISE LAMENT	14200	$2.50
☐ THE DREADFUL LEMON SKY	14148	$2.25
☐ THE EMPTY COPPER SEA	14149	$2.25
☐ THE GREEN RIPPER	14345	$2.50

Buy them at your local bookstore or use this handy coupon for ordering.

COLUMBIA BOOK SERVICE, CBS Publications
32275 Mally Road, P.O. Box FB, Madison Heights, MI 48071

Please send me the books I have checked above. Orders for less than 5 books must include 75¢ for the first book and 25¢ for each additional book to cover postage and handling. Orders for 5 books or more postage is FREE. Send check or money order only. Allow 3-4 weeks for delivery.

Cost $_____   Name _____

Sales tax*_____   Address _____

Postage_____   City _____

Total $_____   State _____ Zip _____

*The government requires us to collect sales tax in all states except AK, DE, MT, NH and OK

Prices and availability subject to change without notice.   8207

More books by John D. MacDonald

☐ **PLEASE WRITE FOR DETAILS**   14080 $2.25

At a Mexican art colony known as the Cuernavaca Summer Work-
shop what goes on and comes off is the stuff a he-man's dreams are
made of . . . a no-money-back, uninhibited, unabridged romp
through passion and Picasso under the naked Mexican sun.

☐ **A MAN OF AFFAIRS**   14051 $2.25

Lost weekends in the Bahamas and enough girls for everyone. Mike
Dean had a use for them—to take other men's minds off their trou-
bles, to bend them to his will. But one of his house guests refused
to see things Mike Dean's way. . . .

More books by John D. MacDonald